Rusty's Repair

A Novel

By Roger K. Droz

Rusty's Repair, A Novel

by Roger K. Droz

Copyright 2021 by Roger K. Droz

ISBN: 978-1-7351760-8-6

Published August 2021

Personal Chapters LLC
Independence, MO and Wakarusa, KS
personalchapters@gmail.com

Table of Contents

FOR MARGO

Without whose patience, support and encouragement, this book would not have happened!

To Anne, Mary Ann, Mary, Nancy,
and Norm,

Thank you.

And to Professor Andrew "Andy" Farkas,
whose inspiration and guidance made this possible.

Chapter 1

*M*y Mama said I was born with a full head of red hair. She said it was the prettiest hair she'd ever seen. She said her daddy had red hair, too, and folks called him "Red." She said she wanted me to have a special name, not just the same as Grandpa's, so she named me Russell. She said she wanted to call me Rusty.

I was born in an old log house on a 30-acre farm on the bank of Cedar Creek in Southeast Iowa about five miles north of Stockport. I hardly knew my Daddy. He left us when I was about three. He wasn't very nice to me. He wasn't very nice to Mama either. About all I remember about him was, he was always yelling. Sometimes yelling at me and sometimes yelling at Mama. Sometimes he'd just be yelling at nothing. But he was always yelling.

One morning when we got up, he was gone. He didn't say goodbye. He just up and left in the middle of the night, took all his clothes and most of our food. Nobody ever saw him again. Nobody missed him either. Mama didn't seem sad about it. In fact, she didn't seem to care a bit that he was gone. She never spoke about him. I never even heard her say his name. Mama threw away the only picture of him we had in the house. I was about seven years old when I first learned his name. That was when I heard old Mr. Webster tell someone I was "Homer and Millie Jordan's kid."

We lived at the end of the lane, just on past Noah Webster's place. Our farm lay on the inside of a bend on Cedar Creek. We had a little two-room log house and a barn. We didn't have running water or electricity. Our outhouse sat at the base of the hill about a hundred feet from the house. Daddy left Mama a couple of milk cows, about 6 hogs, an old mule, and a whole bunch of chickens. We always had cats in the barn, and we had a big brown dog. Mama called him Moose. The cats didn't have names.

Moose didn't do much but lay around. But when a stranger came along, which wasn't very often, Ole Moose would bark and growl like he was mad enough to kill. That was his only job. That and eating, of course. Boy, that dog could eat. He may have had just one job, but he sure was good at it. Strangers never came around again once he scared them off.

Mama didn't have no help. She milked the cows, fed the hogs and chickens all by herself. We had a garden by the house that she planted and picked alone till I was old enough to help. We had some apple and cherry trees too. There were strawberries and blueberries and gooseberries in the woods. Mama dried apples, canned cherries, and made jam from the blueberries and gooseberries. We had potatoes, carrots, beans, corn, and turnips in the root cellar; we never went hungry.

Saturdays we'd ride our mule to Stockport where Mama would sell eggs and butter to the general store. She sold produce in the summer and sometimes a chicken or two when she could spare them.

Our clothes were all hand-me-downs. Some of the ladies in town seemed to like Mama and watched for her to show up on Saturdays. They always had something for "that poor Jordan woman and her boy." Shoes were hard to come by. I never did have a new pair. Once in a while, somebody would give me a pair that they had outgrew. When they did, I wore them till I outgrew them too. After the soles wore out, I'd tie a piece of leather over the holes and wear them some more. Even when I did have shoes, I went barefoot most of the time. Mama said I needed to make my shoes last as long as I could.

We had a wood stove in the middle of the big room. Mama did all her cooking and baking on it. In the winter it was all we had to heat the house.

Old Mr. Webster lived up at the corner where the road split three ways. One way went to Glasgow, one led to Fairfield, and the other to Stockport. Stockport wasn't very big, but it was the closest. That's why we always went there. Besides, Mama didn't like big towns. Mr. Webster had a sawmill on his place. He fixed it up so he could cut wood to build his house. Seemed like he was always cutting wood for one of the neighbors instead of for himself though. He never spent much time working on his own place. He was married but we never did see his wife much at first. She'd be out there hangin' clothes up or workin' in her garden. Sometimes, if it was hot, she'd bring Mr. Webster a drink while he was workin'.

Mr. Webster kept an eye on Mama's woodpile and whenever it started to run low, he'd come driving his team down the hill toward the house with the wagon loaded full up. He'd stack it for us, then leave without saying a word. Mama used to try to give him some eggs or beans or an armload of corn, but he wouldn't ever take anything. He'd say, "I don't need nothing today Millie, maybe next time."

Folks were always bringing logs to Mr. Webster's mill for him to cut. I liked to sneak up there and watch him work. The mill fascinated me. I loved the smell of fresh-cut wood. I would sit and watch the big blade spinning, turning those big tree trunks into slabs of wood. I loved to see the sawdust flying everywhere. He'd drag them big old logs up to the saw with his team of horses, then he used some ropes to finagle the new log up on the table. It was magic, watching him work, seein' his big hands pulling on them levers, makin' them big logs slide back and forth past the big blade. He wasn't near as big as I remember Daddy, but he must have been strong as a bull, 'cuz he sure could muscle them logs. He'd carry them boards, then he'd cut and stack 'em like they weren't nothin.

Some days, if the wind was just right, I could smell that wood clear down to our house. If it was a windy day, a big brown cloud of sawdust rose over the mill's roof. I loved that smell. He'd shoo me off when I got too close, but he always did it with a smile. I think he kind of liked having me there.

He hired a drifter named Pete to help him out. Pete didn't seem to like the farming much, but the Swede was big as an ox and was good help at the mill. It wasn't too long before it was Pete who delivered our wood. He'd just throw it off the wagon into a pile and leave it scattered all over when he was done. Mama didn't seem to care; she was just happy to get the wood. She would offer Pete a big glass of water and maybe some bread and jerky or a piece of apple pie when she had some.

Pete wasn't like Mr. Webster though; he never turned down whatever she offered. It wasn't long before he started showing up in the evening. Most times the wagon would only have half a load, sometimes there wasn't nothing on it at all. Mama didn't mind at first. She'd send me and Moose down to the creek to play and let Pete come in the house.

"Don't you come back till you see the wagon leave," she'd say.

I didn't mind. Me and Moose had some fine times down there together. I'd go climb up on my favorite rock and skip stones on the water. Moose would lay in the sun and do what Moose did best, sleep. Sometimes I'd lay down too. Moose always moved over and curled up beside me when I did.

Moose was my best friend.

Pete started showing up almost every night. It wasn't long before Mama wouldn't go out to meet him anymore. He'd beat on the door till she finally let him in. Mama would tell me not to leave but Pete would drag me to the door and give me a boot on my bottom. He'd say, "git outta here boy. Don't be coming back till you see my wagon's gone."

I'd go down to the creek with Moose. I knew Mama wanted me to stay but I was afraid of Pete.

Most times, after he left, she'd be crying but there wasn't nothin' I could do to make her feel better. Pete was three times bigger than me, and he could get real mean. After he'd leave, she wouldn't let me back in the house for a while. Her face would be red and sometimes she had bruises.

I wanted to tell Mr. Webster but I didn't think he'd believe me. Besides, he was probably afraid of Pete too.

One night in the middle of all the yelling, screaming, and crying, I heard Mama cry, "Don't you understand? I am going to have a baby!"

Then the door flew open, and Pete came storming out. He ran right into me, knocked me down. He jumped up on the wagon and whipped them horses all the way to the top of the hill.

The next morning, early, Mr. Webster came shuffling down the lane. Closest I'd ever seen him come to running. "You seen Pete?" he asked. "He didn't come back to the house last night. The wagon is down by the mill, but the horses and buckboard is gone."

All Mama said was, "He was here for a while, then he left."

I never saw Mama smile again after that. Not ever. From then on, most days, I'd get up, do the chores, make some breakfast, put a sandwich and an apple in my sack and leave for school while she was still in bed.

After school, I'd come back home and work in the garden till chore time. Then I'd do the chores and go to the creek with Moose till dark. When I came in, there was always supper on the stove. I'd fix my plate and try to get Mama to eat with me. She'd just sit and rock. She never said nothin', just sit. She had to be eating something sometime, but she was getting real skinny.

Most nights I went to bed while she sat in her rocker with her Bible on her lap and staring out our window. I wondered why she read that book; it didn't bring her any pleasure.

Most days she'd go all day without ever speaking a word.

She had her baby that winter on about the coldest night I ever seen. She told me it was coming; told me to run up the lane and get Mr. Webster, then hurry back.

When I told Mr. Webster, what was going on, he yelled for his wife, and the three of us high-tailed it back down the hill, the fastest I ever seen them horses run. When he saw what was going on, he left his wife with Mama and hurried to town to get a doctor.

By the time they got back with the doctor, the baby had already come.

Mama had a little girl. Mama named her Janie. Janie had curly blond hair. Mama said she looked just like me, but I didn't think so. Janie cried a lot at first, so Mama spent a lot of time just sitting in the rocker and holding her close.

Having a baby to take care of kind of brought Mama out of her mood some. She had Janie on her hip all the time she was up and around. Now, at least she was cooking and eating every day. Some days she even came out and worked in the garden when I was out there. She'd wrap Janie in a blanket and sit her in a little basket while she worked. Moose took right to Janie. He'd lay next to Janie whenever Mama laid her down. In the evenings, she sat in the rocker with Janie on her knee and the Bible in her lap, and Moose would always lay right beside them. Early spring, we bought another cow from Mr. Webster, she said she needed more milk for the baby. We butchered a hog, so we had bacon and ham with almost every meal.

The first couple of years after Janie was born were good ones. The bins in the barn were full and we had corn and wheat to sell. The root cellar was full of potatoes, onions, carrots, turnips, squash, and such.

We put up carrots and beans, made applesauce and canned some cherries. Saturdays we always had lots of goods to sell in town.

It seemed like it rained every time we needed it. Three years in a row the creek didn't flood, but we always had enough water in our little pond for the stock to drink. I was now ten, finally big enough to work a little for Mr. Webster. He paid me cash money.

For the first time, I had money of my own. I kept it in a little fruit jar under my bed and every night I counted it before I went to sleep.

Janie was growing fast. She sure was pretty, too. That pretty face with those green eyes and curly hair made me smile every time I looked at her. She'd got over all that bawling she used to do. She'd smile at me every time I got close. Mama'd let me hold her a lot and once Janie learned to walk a little, she'd try to follow me around all the time. I didn't mind though; it was nice having someone to take care of and talk to, cuz Mama still didn't talk much.

We bought a horse from a farmer down the road toward Glasgow. Mr. Webster told us about him. He took Mama to see it, then he rode it home while Mama drove the wagon. She looked all proud, coming down the lane, driving the team, following Mr. Webster on our new horse. He was a big thing, kind of red looking, 'bout the color of my hair. Mama named him Sam. She said Sam was broke to ride, so's we wouldn't have to walk to town no more.

We didn't have no saddle, just a bridle, and reins, so I'd ride Sam bareback. Sam was a good horse. He'd just stand in his pen all day when we weren't using him, and go in the barn at night, or when the weather was bad. Mr. Webster put a gate in the fence between him and us. We could let Sam out in his pasture to eat and hang out with the workhorses.

We began to enjoy Sundays. Sometimes Mama would pack up a basket with some food. I would put her and Janie up on Sam and lead them down along the creek to the meadow. Sometimes when it was nice, we all went down to the swimming hole where some of the neighbors gathered. Sometimes we would go to the church; when we did, we always sat in back though. We never got there in time to go in with everyone else and we always left before the service was over. I think Mama didn't want to talk to the preacher. Mama watched Janie play with the other girls after church, but she never talked to any of the other mothers.

Mama still never smiled.

I never did like school much. Most all the kids started afore me, so I was always behind on everything. I didn't understand numbers and how they worked. I couldn't read good, like the rest of the kids and the teacher always had to help me understand the hard parts. All the other kids would giggle and whisper while she was helping me. They all had nicer clothes than me, too. None of them was ever nice to me, so I never made friends out of any of them. Mama told me I had to go. "School is gonna help you out when you get to be a man," she'd say. So I trudged up there and back every day. Still, I didn't see the use.

Janie started school as soon as she was old enough. I'd walk her there and back every day. She'd never been around anyone but me and Mama, so she was happy to meet new kids. Every day was a new adventure for her. She had friends for the first time ever. The other kids were nice to her, always asking her to play. It didn't bother her that they all had more than she did.

I still struggled to get through each day with my own learning.

While we were gone to school, Mama stayed home alone. She'd didn't do much, just sit around and dwell on the past, I guess. I think the bad memories were getting to be too much for her. Thinking about all the stuff that had happened to her, first with Daddy and then Pete. She'd gone back to sitting in her rocker with her Bible on her lap all the time.

Janie couldn't understand why Mama changed. She'd crawl up on Mama's lap to tell her all about school, but Mama would just sit there and stare off most times. Sometimes she acted like she didn't know that Janie was even there.

The walks to school started getting hard for me. I didn't like it there and I didn't like leaving Mama alone. Janie kept asking me what was wrong with Mama and I couldn't tell her, cuz I didn't know. Janie's questions were endless and I didn't have any answers.

Fridays were Janie's favorite school days. She couldn't wait to get home and see Mama. She'd have stories to tell about what all the other kids did. How they was going to church or a picnic, how they'd git to go shopping or go see some of their families who lived off somewhere.

Janie looked forward to our Saturday trips to town and the Sunday picnics with friends at the swimming hole or the churchyard. Sometimes she'd end up crying because Mama didn't seem to care about all her stories.

This one Friday, the walk home started like all the others. She laughed and skipped all the way to Mr. Webster's corner. She was going so fast it was hard for me to keep up. She couldn't wait to tell Mama about her day. She waited for me to catch up at the edge of the road, then pulled heavy on my hand until we got to the gate, then she let go and ran ahead for the house. I just trotted along behind, figuring there wasn't a need to hurry. From the lane, I watched as she burst through the door and into the house. But in seconds she was back outside the door, yelling, "Mama's not here!"

"Go look in the garden," I called.

In a flash, Janie disappeared through the garden gate. Next, I saw her run toward the barn. Then back to the front of the house.

"She's not in the garden. I looked in the barn, too. She's not there either," she cried.

I knew something was wrong. It wasn't like Mama to not be here. I yelled to Janie, "Run up to Mr. Webster's and see if she's there." I knew Mama wasn't going to be there. She hadn't been to Mr. Webster's place since Pete left, but I knew something wasn't right and I wanted to be the first to see what it was.

After Janie left, I climbed the hill to Grandpa Red and Grandma Pearl's graves. Mama went there sometimes to be alone. I used to see her up there talking to them like they were still alive.

Mama wasn't there either.

The cows and Sam were in the barn, so I knew she wasn't out in the field.

The creek was the only place left to look.

Soon as I started down there, I saw Moose sitting on our favorite rock. I yelled for him, but he didn't turn around. He'd never done that before. Something about the creek made me all sick inside. I wished Mr. Webster was here. I didn't want to go on alone, but I couldn't stop, I had to see what was bothering Moose.

As I got closer, I could see something floating in the water. It was Mama. She had on her Sunday dress and was floating face down in the creek. A stream of blood was coming from her body. Streaks of red were beginning to cover the whole pool.

I sat down on the rock next to Moose. He looked up with those big sad eyes and whimpered when I put my hand on his shoulders. We sat there, quiet for a minute, then I felt a strange peace come over me, sitting there and looking. I felt a sense of quiet inside, kind of a relief.. sort of. I knew Mama wasn't ever going to suffer anymore.

We buried Mama next to Grandpa and Grandma. Nobody was at the service except the preacher, Janie, me, and Mr. and Mrs. Webster. The preacher used Mama's Bible to speak from and Mr. Webster had a stone carved. It said, "Here lies Janice Jordan, mother of Rusty and Janie."

I put Mama's Bible on the shelf with the only two other books she owned–books she used to read to me–*The Adventures of Tom Sawyer*, and *Little Women.* After they all left, I put Mama's bed and rocker on the burn pile, covered it with brush, and lit it all on fire. I watched it burn until I couldn't see it anymore because of my tears. Then Janie and me went back to the house. I fixed supper and we went to bed.

Janie cried all night.

Chapter 2

*W*e were all alone now, Janie and me. Taking care of Janie and the place was up to me now. School got harder than ever; the only reason I went was so she would go too. She cried every night till she couldn't cry anymore before she fell to sleep.

Moose died. I found him early one morning, laying in the spot where Mama's rocking chair sat.

He'd been acting like he missed Mama too. He'd lay where Mama's rocker used to be for hours. Lots of times, he wouldn't even follow me outside. He was never around when I did chores or worked in the garden. I couldn't even get him to go with me to the creek, but I didn't like going there much anymore. When I did go, I'd look at that spot where I found Mama and start crying.

I think Ole Moose probably died of a broken heart. I buried him up in our cemetery, at her feet, jest like he used to lay. I think Mama would have liked that.

I started not caring so much about things after that. Weeds started taking over the garden. Potatoes needed dug but I didn't dig 'em. Corn needed picking; I didn't pick it either. Squash was out there rotting on the vine. All I did was milk the cows and feed the animals. I couldn't even drag myself up to the sawmill.

I still walked Janie to school every day, but I quit going in. Most times, I didn't even go back to the house after I left her. I'd spend the day walking, maybe just up the road or in the woods across from Mr. Webster's. I'd go to get Janie in the afternoon and walk her home. She'd squeeze my hand all the way there and back. Some days she didn't say a word all the time we walked. I didn't neither.

One day the teacher was waiting outside when we got there and she asked me what was wrong.

"Nothin'."

Then she asked Janie.

Janie started bawling, "My Mama died!"

The teacher didn't say any more, she just took Janie's hand and led her inside the school.

Every day after that, Janie's teacher was waiting at the gate when we arrived. She always took Janie's hand to lead her. She always asked me to come too.

"Rusty, I wish you would come with us. You need to be around the other kids. It's not right for a twelve-year-old boy to be alone like this."

I'd try to smile when I answered, "I'm sorry, ma'am, I can't."

Chapter 3

I was milking our cow when I heard the car. From out the barn door, I could see it stop short of the mud hole. It couldn't go any farther.

We had a low place in our lane, about four feet wide, that only dried out when it hadn't rained for a long time. Mr. Webster had helped me make a little walking bridge over it so we could get past it without getting mud on our feet. He cut two cedar trees into logs to lay across, and he and I laid them across the mud. Then he cut some pieces of oak into planks for the walkway. Then the next time he brought wood to Mama he brought the planks too. He showed me how to set the planks, then drill and peg each one to the cedar trusses. He grinned as he watched me set the rest of them. He told Mama, "Rusty sure did a good job of making that bridge." My bridge was only wide enough to walk on, and not nearly big enough for a car. It was all we needed though, because we never had a car.

I walked to the barn door to see what was going on. A man and woman got out of their car and started walking toward the house. She had on a blue dress that was buttoned up to her neck. She was wearing city shoes with pointy heels. He had on a brown suit that wasn't big enough for him. He was a big man, but he was soft and blubbery. He didn't look like he could do much work. They walked up and beat on our door. Janie didn't open it because I told her to never answer if strangers came. Shortly, the man and woman saw me standing off and walked over.

The woman spoke first, "Is this the Jordan place?"

"Yup," I said.

"What's your name, son?" she asked.

"Folks call me Rusty."

"Do you have a sister named Jane?"

"Her name is Janie," I said.

"Is she here?" the woman asked.

I glanced over to where Janie was now standing in the door of the house, watching us. They both saw her, so I called for her to come on out.

"We are from the state children's care department. We understand your mother died and you two live here alone," the man said.

"Yup, just the two of us. We're doin' just fine," I said.

"We have come to help you find a new home," he told me.

"We don't need no new home. This here is our home. We like it here just fine."

But just as soon as Janie got close, the lady grabbed her arm and pulled her away.

Janie started screaming, "I don't want to go to no new home. I want to stay here with Rusty!"

"Rusty is coming with us," he answered.

I tried to pull Janie back away from her, but the big man grabbed me and pushed me down. He took hold of Janie's other arm and the two of them dragged her toward the car.

He looked back and yelled, "Stay here, we'll be right back for you!"

They locked Janie in the backseat of their car. I could see her in the window beating on the glass, screaming, and crying. The big man turned and headed back toward me. His face was red now, he had sweat running down his cheeks and his eyes were on fire. The woman was stumbling along behind, trying to hurry, struggling as best she could to keep up in her city dress and those city shoes.

I didn't want to go to a new home, but I didn't want to leave Janie. The big man was bearing down on me. The city lady was yelling from behind him. I could hear Janie screaming and yelling my name. I didn't know what to do.

Just before the big man could get hold of me, I panicked and ran.

I didn't want to, but I couldn't think. I didn't want to run, but I did. I knew the big man couldn't run fast enough to catch me and I knew they couldn't find me once I crossed the creek. If I could get up the hill, I could stop and think.

I ran for the creek.

The big man came running after me like a big dumb cow. I heard him fall and lose his wind. I looked back and saw him layin' on the ground. He didn't run very far and fell again; this time I could tell he was hurt. He lay there moaning and cursing. I heard the woman yelling, "Get up you big slob, the kid is getting away!" He didn't move. They yelled at each other for a bit, and then he limped back to where she was holding Janie in the car.

I ran to the ford, crossed the creek, and scrambled up the bank on the other side. From the top of the hill, I could see them limping back to their car, dragging a screaming Janie between them. From up on the hill I could see Janie in the backseat, frantically beating on the window as they got in their car and backed all the way up to Mr. Webster's corner. I lay there and watched until their dust cloud finally disappeared.

I knew they would come back again tomorrow.

At dusk, I sneaked back down, and fed and watered the stock, and milked the cows. Then I took a blanket, some water, a couple of potatoes, and some jerky from the cellar and climbed back up the hill for the night.

I didn't get much sleep, sobbing, worrying, and wondering about Janie.

I got up before dawn, went down, and did the chores. I didn't want to go back, but Sam and the hogs needed fed and the cows had to be milked. When I finished, I took some more food from the cellar and climbed back up the hill.

Sure enough, they came back about mid-morning.

I lay in the weeds and watched as they searched for about an hour, then left again.

I lay up there in the sun all day, thinking. I didn't have any idea about what to do. Just before dusk, I climbed back down, did the chores, and took some more supplies.

They came back again the next day, looked for a while, and left. I couldn't quite hear what they were saying, but I knew they were about to give up. This time when they left, I tried to follow them, but by the time I got to Mr. Webster's corner, they were out of sight and I couldn't tell which way they went. I was desperate to find out where they took Janie, so I went back to the barn and saddled Sam. I followed the creek downstream a ways, then cut across a field toward Stockport. I turned south, riding the back ways along the edge of woods and through gullies. When I got to town, I followed the alley to the General Store and knocked on the back door.

Mr. Kerr finally came to the door to see who was making all the racket. "What on earth do you want, Rusty?" he asked.

"They took Janie and I need to find her!" I cried.

"What are you talking about? Who took Janie? Calm down son, and tell me what is going on," he said.

I told him all about the man and the woman who took Janie. I told him how they came back for me but couldn't find me. I told him I needed to find out what happened to Janie. I told him I had to get her back.

"Well, one thing's for sure; they didn't bring her here. There aren't any people in Stockport that do that kind of thing. Maybe they took her down to Keosauqua, maybe up to Fairfield," he said.

I'd never been to Keosauqua before. I wasn't even sure where it was. I'd never been to Fairfield either, but I knew one of the roads at Mr. Webster's corner went that way.

"Where should I go?" I asked.

Your best bet is to go to Fairfield. I don't think there's anyone in Keosauqua that would do such a thing as steal a child. I'll ask the guy from Keosauqua that brings me feed. He's due in this afternoon. He might know something. I'll pass the word around town and if anyone knows anything, they'll tell me. I'll pass anything I learn to Noah Webster. I have customers that go to his sawmill."

I climbed on Sam and pointed him toward home. He knew the way, so I sat and let him lead. He walked up to the barnyard gate and stood with his head down, waiting as I slid off. I slipped off his saddle and bridle and watched him plod into his stall. It seemed like he knew something was wrong. I spent another night up on the bluff, watching the house and sobbing. In the morning after sneaking into the house and fixing breakfast, I saddled Sam up again and we rode up the hill. I stopped at Mr. Webster's. I forgot I hadn't told him anything about all this.

"I ain't seen hide nor hair of anyone, let alone a city couple. There haven't been any strangers hanging around, that I know of," Mr. Webster said.

So me and Sam picked the Fairfield road and set out to look for her.

It took me most of the morning just to get there. I tied Sam to a tree by a stream, fed him some oats, and walked the rest of the way to look around. Fairfield had some big buildings there, bigger than any in Stockport, but I couldn't read the signs on the front of any of 'em. For the first time, I wished I had learned more in school.

I was walking down the street, looking at stores when a nice lady stopped to ask me my name and if I needed help. I didn't tell her my real name, I told her, "My name's Tom." It was all I could think of to say. Then I said, "I'm looking for a place where they keep little kids."

She started asking me a bunch of questions like, where was I from, who I was looking for, why was I looking. I didn't know what I should say or not say, so I panicked and ran again. She called after me like she wanted to help, but I kept running. I found some barrels in an alley, scrunched down behind them, and watched her until she finally walked away. Once I was sure she wasn't going to turn around, I followed her to a big building where some man in a uniform came out and talked to her. I hid behind a tree and watched her; she was pointing over to where I had just been. Then she led the man to that spot. They talked some more, and she left, then he started to look around. They walked back to the big building; he went in and she walked on down the street. I waited for a while, the man didn't come back out, so I sneaked over to the building and looked in the window. He was sitting in there alone with a bunch of papers on his desk so I figured it was safe to look around some more.

I spent the rest of the daylight going up and down alleys and looking in windows. I couldn't find any place where it looked like they might keep kids, so I crawled under a porch to hide and fell asleep. The sun was low when I woke. I hurried to where I left poor Sam, climbed on, and trotted home. I felt bad for leaving him all day. After I watered Sam good, I gave him an extra scoop of oats once I put him in the barn.

I spent the next few days doin' chores in the morning and at night, sleeping on top of the cliff. Me and Sam spent the daylight riding to town and looking for Janie. Sunday I sneaked down to the meadow to watch the picnickers. A couple of the girls Janie liked were down by the creek so I sneaked down there to talk to them.

"We asked the teacher how come Janie wasn't in school and she said she didn't know," Janie's best friend said.

"A man and a woman took her. They put her in their car and drove off. I've been looking all over for her," I told them.

I saw two of their mothers coming toward us. The girls weren't any help to me, and I didn't want to have to tell their mothers, so I ran along the creek bank toward home.

I spent the next couple of days just thinking. I didn't know where else to look for Janie. I couldn't go back to the school 'cuz I figured they was watching for me up in Fairfield. Sam and I had been back to Stockport twice. Mr. Kerr didn't have any news and I was starting to think he wouldn't be able to find anything out for me. I knew I couldn't stay home 'cuz sooner or later they would be back looking for me. All I could think to do was just run away. I didn't want to, but there wasn't anything else to do.

Early the next morning, before chores, I drove the livestock up to the gate that connected our field to Mr. Webster's, opened it, and herded them through. I hated to leave Sam but figured I couldn't take good care of him if I took him with me, so he'd be better off at Mr. Webster's. I knew the cows and pigs would find their way to his barn. I knew when Mr. Webster found them, he would know what I'd done.

I got my money jar from under the bed, rolled up my extra pants and shirt in a blanket, and packed up all the food I could carry in an old gunny sack. It took me a while to get started. I stood in the doorway of the house for the longest time, looking around. Janie's clothes were still stacked up over in her corner. All her dolls was laying on her bed, just where she put them the last time she made her bed. I picked up her favorite doll and held it for a while. I wanted to take it with me, but somehow it didn't seem the right thing to do. I put it back on the bed with her other three dolls, pulled the covers up over them, and for some reason, picked up Mama's Bible.

I crossed the creek and climbed the bank.

I stood on top of the hill. I tried not to look back but couldn't help it. Down there sat my farm, the only place I ever lived, the only place I ever knew.

I could see our cows and hogs up in Mr. Webster's pasture. Sam was standing with the draft horses, looking like he was watching for me to come down the hill. Like he was expecting me to come get him. I knew I would never see Janie again. I knew I would never see our farm again. I knew I would never see Mr. Webster and his sawmill again.

That's all I knew.

Chapter 4

I started south. I'd heard of Missouri but had never been there. I figured that since I'd never been there and nobody there knew me, no one would come looking for me there.

I followed fencerows and ditches and stayed off roads so no one would see me. I walked all day until I got to a town where I had to cross a river. I couldn't find no place shallow enough to wade so I'd have to wait until dark to cross on the bridge. I hid under the bridge and waited till it was dark enough, but every time I climbed up the bank to cross, a car or a wagon would come over. It took me several tries, but once I made it, I spent the rest of the night laying on top of the hill, looking back down on the river. It was a lot like the bluff on the Cedar above our farm. I spent the whole rest of the night thinking about Janie, Mama, Moose, Sam, and Mr. Webster. It was a cold clear night. There were millions of stars in the sky. I lay there looking at the same sky that Moose and I watched from my rock back home. My thoughts made me sick inside.

A rooster woke me up. There was frost on the ground. I was cold. I was hungry and thirsty too. Most of all, I was all alone.

I picked up my stuff and headed south. I hadn't walked too long, and I saw a road sign. I couldn't make out what it said, but one of the big words started with an "M". I figured it must say Missouri. I walked for at least five more miles before I figured I was probably safe in Missouri. I got on a gravel road and walked on. I found a tree stump on the edge of the road and decided to sit a spell. My head was spinning. I should have said goodbye to Mr. Webster, told him why I turned our livestock out in his field. He's been so good to me and Janie and Mama. I ought to go back to Fairfield again, just in case Janie is there. I wonder if Mr. Kerr ever found anything out? If I keep going south, I probably don't have any chance of ever seeing Janie again.

I climbed down off the stump, walked back to the road, and started north. I had to go back.

I don't know why, but I walked along the shoulder of the road. I didn't meet many cars and the few that passed me waved but didn't stop. I watched for them that were going the same way I was and hid in the ditch as they passed. I didn't want anyone trying to give me a ride. I didn't want to have to answer a bunch of questions about what I was doing out here and where I was going.

I walked right across the bridge I had been under the night before and right into that town. There was a little park with some picnic tables, a slide, and a swing. There was a pump under a little roof, so I filled my water bottle. Then I mustered up my courage and went inside a store.

"What can I get for you?" asked the man behind the meat counter.

"I want a cold sandwich and something to drink," I answered.

"What kind of sandwich?" he asked.

"Whatever's good," I answered. I never bought anything like this in a store before.

He smiled, "I never seen you around here before. What's your name and where you from, son?"

"Folks call me Rusty," I blurted. "I've been down in Missouri seeing my uncle."

"Are you walking?" he asked.

"No sir, I'm riding my horse. I left him tied over at the water tank," I lied.

He piled a whole bunch of meat on a piece of bread, "You want any cheese or mustard on it?"

"No sir, just plain will be fine," I answered. I had never tasted mustard before.

He wrapped my sandwich in a piece of paper and put it in a bag, wrote something on the bag, and handed it over the counter. "We've got Orange and Grapette soda in the cooler," he said. "Help yourself to whichever you want. Do you have any money?"

"Yes sir," I said, and began to pull my money bag out of my pack.

"Well, you just tell Hazel upfront to charge you a dime."

"Thank you, sir."

"You be careful out there, son," he said and smiled down at me.

I gave Hazel a dime.

She smiled and gave me a nickel in change. "Sandwiches are on special today," she said.

There was a bench out front of the store and those picnic tables over in the park. I didn't want anyone seeing me and I didn't want anybody asking questions, so I walked back to the road and climbed down under the bridge with my food.

The man at the store put more meat in my sandwich than Mama ever put on the table for me and her and Janie at supper. I took more than half out, wrapped it up in the paper, and put it back in the bag. Once I finished eating, I leaned back on my pack to finish my soda and watch the water run by. I'm not for sure how long I slept, but the shadows were getting long when I woke. I had figured on getting at least back to Stockport by nightfall, so I climbed up onto the road and lit out walking as fast as I could.

It was beginning to get dark as I was getting close to Stockport. I wanted to talk to Mr. Kerr about Janie before I went on, so I figured I'd stay there for the night and talk to him in the morning. I made me a little hidey-hole behind some boxes by his backdoor, pulled my jacket up, and settled in.

The next thing I knew, someone was making a racket out front. I pulled my jacket down off my head and looked out. The sun was already pretty high up. I hadn't slept that hard in I don't know how long. Mr. Kerr was happy to see me. He took me to the back of the store and fixed me a plate with some cold chicken, a boiled egg, and a big glass of milk. I ate more food in the last two meals than I usually ate in three or four days. Mr. Kerr didn't have any news for me though. He said, "My feed guy was here just after you left. He didn't know anything about any missing kids, or anybody who was stealing them. He said he'd pass the word around. He has a lot of other towns on his route, so if Janie's anywhere close, chances are he might find out."

"I'm going on back to the farm, then on to Fairfield, after that, I don't know. Maybe you could write your mailing address down for me, so's I could have someone write to you for me?"

"I'll be watching for Janie," he said. "Come on back anytime you need to. If there is ever anything I can do for you, all you have to do is ask." He reached down to shake my hand.

We both held on for a long time.

I made it back to our farm about noon. Then I laid on the hill above, bawling like a little kid, trying to think about what to do. The livestock was all up in Mr. Webster's field. I could see Sam up there with the work-horses. They was standing close to the gate between our place and Mr. Webster's. Sam seemed to be looking down toward the barn like he was wondering or thinking about what was going on. I finally decided there wasn't any point in going down there so I walked the meadow and up the hill toward Mr. Webster's. Sam saw me and came running. He wouldn't leave me alone so I jumped on and rode him round the pasture for a while. Mr. Webster's two workhorses followed us all around. The fuss we stirred up 'caused Mr. Webster to come out of his sawmill. When he saw it was me, he came running. I was planning to tell him about everything that happened, so I climbed down and walked Sam up to him.

We went back to the sawmill and sat.

"I seen Sam and your stock in the field the other morning. I figured you lit out. Didn't know if I'd ever see you again. How come you come back? What ya figure on doin' now?" he asked.

"I jest couldn't stand it down there at the house alone no more," I said. "I was headed south, don't know where I was goin', jest south. I got down into Missouri and got to thinkin' bout Janie, and just had to come back. I want to go back to Fairfield and look some more. But if I don't find her or come up with no leads, I don't know what I'll do."

"You hungry? I'll have the missus fix you a plate. You stay here tonight. Tomorrow, we'll drive the team to town. The missus, she's got some tradin' she's been wantin' to do anyways."

"No thanks, I just ate at Mr. Kerr's in Stockport. Think I'll go back down to the house, maybe put some flowers on Mama's grave, clean the place up a bit and sleep in the barn," I told him.

"Well, come on back up for breakfast, we'll go to town," he pleaded.

I watched him walk back toward his house real slow. I sat there on the stack of wood for a bit thinking.

I could stay here. I figure he's gonna ask me to tomorrow. He don't have no help since Pete lit out. But if I can't find Janie here, I ain't gonna be able to stand livin' right next to the home place without her.

I cleaned up the graves, then I went down by the creek and dug one of those little maple trees that are so pretty in the fall. I brought it up and planted it just south of Mama's, Grandpa Red's, Grandma's, and Moose's graves. It'll be nice when it grows some. Give them some shade on them hot July and August afternoons. I let Sam through the gate. He was up there pawing and whinnying so much. I figured he and I could sleep together in the barn one last time. No way was I going back in the house.

All those years I'd lived down below, Mrs. Webster had been nice to me, but I didn't see her much. She had talked to Mama some, but she'd never said much to me.

When I got there in the morning, she already had a big breakfast fixed– bacon and eggs, fresh biscuits, sausage gravy, and a bowl of strawberries. All this was laid out on a clean white tablecloth. Mama didn't even have a tablecloth. Neither she nor Mr. Webster said much as we sat; they just watched me eat. Once we were done Mrs. Webster cleaned off the table and put stuff away. Mr. Webster just sits there drinking his coffee. I knew he was pondering. Shortly, he said, "Well, guess we better be gettin'. Ma, she's got a lot of tradin' to do today. It's probably gonna be dark by the time we git back home."

I knew he wasn't talking about trading; he was talking about me.

It took us about a couple of hours to get to town. I sat between the Websters all the way. They both just sat in his truck, looking straight ahead. I guess I knew what they were thinking, and they knew I was thinking the same thing about them.

Mr. Webster dropped Mrs. Webster off at a grocery store, then started on up the street. "Where we goin'?" I asked.

"We're goin' to the police station or sheriff's office, if they have one, then to the courthouse after," he answered.

This was a good time to talk about it, so I told him all about me sneaking up here, looking for Janie, talking to the lady, and having the policeman come looking for me.

"Don't make no difference," he said. "We're goin' down there now and yer goin' with me. Nobody's gonna' give you no trouble."

The policeman told us there weren't any reports of runaways and until there was, "There's nothing we can do."

Mr. Webster was getting mad and he told the policeman, "Well, I'm tellin' you now, that little girl ain't no runaway, she was stolen. So now you know, and you best get to doin' something."

The policeman got mad, too. "You better get over to the courthouse, talk to the sheriff, they's the ones who can help. This happened in the county, it ain't city business."

We found the sheriff's office and he was in. Mr. Webster started telling all about the couple that'd come to the farm, took Janie, and tried to get Rusty, too. He made it sound like he was taking care of Janie and me after Mama died. So the sheriff didn't get any idea that we were living alone. He seemed nice about it all. "Let's go out front and talk to the secretary. She sees all that paperwork. She might be able to help," he said.

The secretary's name was Belle. She seemed friendly, she said, "We don't have any records about anybody from the schools or folks down here from the state government in Des Moines taking children out of their homes and moving them to orphanages. We did get a letter a few weeks ago from down in Missouri. It was from the Attorney General's office. It was talking about some folks from down around Springfield that they thought were stealing children and babies. It said they ran an orphanage and people were getting suspicious about how many children they had available for adoption. It said to keep a lookout for them, but it didn't give any descriptions," she said.

"I'm real sure that if your daughter turns up down there, we'll hear about it. Did you say Janie was your daughter or granddaughter, Mr. Webster?" she asked.

Mr. Webster didn't answer; he just said, "Well, guess we'll be getting along. Janie must not be around these parts. Have the sheriff get ahold of me if something comes up. I live out southeast of town on the Glasgow road, down where the gravel breaks off toward Stockport."

Mrs. Webster had a pile of goods to load up when we got back to the general store. Mr. Webster and I loaded it all in the back of his truck and started back toward his place. They were both quiet for a long time before Mrs. Webster said, "Rusty, me and Pa want you to live with us. You can work your farm and stay at our house. You're big enough now to help Pa. He can use some help running the mill. We've got a room we don't use; you could move all your stuff in there, bring anything up from your place you want. We're both getting older now and we never had any children. Someday, if you want, the place can be yours."

Mr. Webster looked down at me and smiled. I knew he'd be happy to have me living there.

"I'm sorry ma'am, but I need to keep lookin' for Janie, and if she ain't 'round here, I need to go somewhere else to look," I said.

They both looked away, out the truck windows, and we all got quiet again. No one said any more until we got back to the house. We unloaded all the stuff. I helped put it up and then said, "I'm gonna go down, sleep in the barn tonight. I'll be leavin' first light."

"You come up to the house before you go," Mr. Webster said sternly. I could tell he didn't think there was any point trying to get me to change my mind about leaving. "We'll have some food packed and waitin'."

I left Sam up there in Mr. Webster's barn and walked down the hill alone. I knew if I took him with me, he would cause a commotion all night so I didn't want him staying in the barn with me. Sam seemed to know I was leaving and I knew if he was in the barn with me, it'd be hard not to change my mind.

The next morning, I packed my clothes back in my bag and walked up the hill for what I thought would be the last time.

"There's some jerky and dried apples in the bag. Some fruit and berries in a little bag. I put a couple of new pairs of socks in there too. A little money tied up too," Mr. Webster said.

"Thank you, sir, but I've got some money," I answered.

"Well, you've got a little more now," he said. Then he got kind of weepy, "I'm gonna miss you, Rusty. I wish you weren't leavin', but I ain't gonna stop you. Remember, you've always got a place here if you ever want to come back. And that money I told you about in the root cellar is still hid and always will be." Then he reached out his hand and took mine, "Good luck to you, son."

We stood there a bit, him holding onto my hand, not wanting to let go; he let loose, and turned toward the house, and began to walk. I could see Mrs. Webster in the window, waving. She was wiping tears off her cheeks. Tears was running down mine too.

Chapter 5

*T*he sun beat down on me from a clear, bright blue sky. The heat rose to swallow me as I walked. The road seemed endless, and I guess it was, because I didn't even have a destination. But there wasn't anything behind me to go back for, so I walked on. When I saw a farmhouse with a well, I would stop and ask for a drink. People all seemed friendly down here in Missouri. Most asked me where I was from and where I was going. A lot of them asked me my name. I couldn't tell them where I was going because I didn't know and I didn't dare give them my name. I didn't like this, never telling any of them the truth. Sometimes they would offer me food. Several ladies insisted that I come in and eat a meal. Some even tried to get me to wash up. Every time I stopped, I'd leave with more stuff than I had when I arrived. Women would make me take some food or maybe a hat or shirt. One lady insisted I take a pair of her husband's boots. Dogs would trot alongside me for a while like they were guarding me from something. Farmers would stop and offer me a ride in the back of their truck or hay rack.

I walked on the shoulder of gravel roads. I figured nobody was looking for me now since I wasn't being missed by anybody but the Websters, and maybe the people that stole Janie. But I was pretty sure they'd moved on to somewhere else. Most people who drove past me smiled and waved. Some stopped to give me a drink or a scrap of food. I didn't let any cars come up behind me though. I'd step off the road when I heard them coming, then watch them go by before I stepped back on. I didn't want any surprises.

Days went by walking in the hot sun. Nights I spent sleeping under bridges or in a woods back off the road. Sometimes folks would let me stay in their haymows. I always got enough handouts so I didn't have to spend any of my own money. Every day when I got up, I'd keep walking south. I didn't know where I was going, I just knew that south would take me farther away. I did kind of have Springfield in my mind though.

I couldn't let go of what that lady at the sheriff's office told me about that adoption place.

One day I heard a truck behind me and stepped off to let it go by. It was a big truck–one of those that pull a big trailer. I watched from the ditch as it whizzed by. Then it stopped a little ways up the road and just sat. I waited a bit, but it didn't start up, so I figured the driver was going to give me a ride so I hurried up to where it sat. Once I got up beside it, the driver leaned out and asked, "Need a ride?"

I smiled, opened the door, and climbed in. We started without him saying a word and rode along in silence for quite a while. He seemed a little strange somehow. I didn't feel good about getting in with him. I wished I had stayed back when he stopped.

Finally, he spoke, "What's yer name, boy?" he asked me.

I didn't think I should tell him straight, so I said, "Name's Randy, sir."

"Well, then Randy, where ya headed?" he asked.

"I'm goin' down a piece to see my uncle, sir," I said.

"Kinda young to be out here travelin' by yerself, ain't ya?" he said.

"I'm gonna be fourteen in a couple of months," I told him.

I didn't ask any questions. I didn't see any need to know his name or anything about him.

He didn't say any more until he slowed and pulled into a field.

"What're we stopping here for?" I asked.

"We gonna have us some fun, boy," the man answered with a mean grin.

I was thinking maybe I should jump out, but before I could, he grabbed hold of my arm and pulled me over against him. I tried to work free, but he was a lot stronger than me. We scuffled and he hit me several times. I couldn't break his grip, but I did manage to get my knife from my pocket with my free hand. Right away he saw I had it and grabbed for it. When his hand hit my arm I lost my grip on my knife and it flew out the open window. His arm was in front of me, trying to grab my free hand, so I leaned forward and bit him hard on his forearm. He screamed and cussed and yelled, "I'm gonna kill you for that, boy."

We really started scuffling then. In all the commotion, I managed to get my other arm free. I grabbed the door handle and was out of that truck in a flash. I ran across a field and was almost to the woods before he ever even got out of his truck. He jumped down and was running after me, but I had a good head start and he couldn't run nearly as fast as I could, so I was getting farther away. He only ran a little bit, then stopped. He was standing back there cursing and screaming just like the fat man that tried to catch me when they took Janie.

"I'll be waitin' up the road for you boy. I'm gonna get you if'n it's the last thing I do," he screamed.

He stood for a bit, holding his arm. I watched from behind a tree in the woods as he crawled back in the cab of his truck. I could see him in there wrapping his arm. Shortly he started the engine, backed back out on the road, sat there a few moments, then drove away. I heard the truck stop just after he got over the hill. I knew he was up there, waiting to see if I showed up so I sat tight. Pretty soon I heard the truck start running again, then I heard it drive off.

It wasn't until I saw the dust from the truck disappearing that I realized that my food, clothes, Mama's Bible, and my money was still laying there on his seat. I didn't dare go back to the road for fear that he might be stopped somewhere ahead. I went back to the edge of the field and followed fence rows and creeks for a while. Now, I didn't have anything but the clothes I had on. I hid there on the edge of the field behind a tree for a bit, trying to think, when I realized my legs were burning. I pulled up a pants legs to look. My legs were all scratched from stumbling through some rose brambles in the field when I was running from the truck.

I walked further into the woods until I found a place where some water was pooled up in a small creek. I sat down on a rock and washed my legs off with my handkerchief the best I could, but that didn't help the burning much. I drank a little of that water too - it tasted pretty bad, but that didn't matter. I didn't have anything else to drink.

I found a tree stump and huddled up for the night. Cattle were roaming in the woods and it wasn't long until they discovered me. They stood there, staring at me, snorting, and mooing low. I didn't get much sleep. I was cold, my legs burnt, the cattle surrounded me and I was worried about what I was going to do next.

The next morning I found a different pond where the water was clearer. It tasted a lot better than the creek. I found some berries to eat too. But I was still afraid to head back out, so I spent all day, watching and worrying. I went back to that same stump and spent a second night.

In the morning I figured the coast was finally clear, so I walked out to the road and started south again. I walked all day without seeing a farmhouse with a well or anyone out working in their fields or garden, no one around to offer me any food or drink. I was tired, hungry, and lonesome. This was about the lowest I ever felt.

The sun was starting to get low and my will to push on was almost gone. I told myself that when I got to the top of the next hill I was going to stop and rest no matter what. From there I didn't know what I would do. I didn't have no place to go, either forward or backward. It was a real long hill, and it was hard to keep going, I tried to just keep putting one foot in front of the other. I was ready to give up. Several times I stopped and just stood in the road. But for some reason, each time I'd start back walking.

Once I finally got to the crest, I stepped off the road and collapsed in the ditch. I laid there for a while, with my eyes shut, before I sat up and began to look around. At the top of the next hill, I saw a couple of buildings in the evening haze. They seemed so far away, but at least they were maybe a place to stop, maybe get some help, and I sure didn't have a reason to keep laying there.

The sun was falling below the horizon when I reached the buildings. There was an old church on one side and a general store on the other. The church was all dark and deserted, but there was a light in the store.

I figured I didn't have anything to lose, so I stepped up on the porch of the store and knocked on the door.

No one answered.

I knocked again.

Still, I didn't hear any noise from inside.

There was an old rocking chair sitting there on the porch. It looked so comfortable, I wanted to collapse in it, but it wouldn't do no good to sit.

I knocked again.

Chapter 6

*T*he rickety old door gave a screech and moan as it slowly opened. A kindly old lady appeared. She just stood, looking down at me for a moment. I could tell by her troubled expression, I must have looked a sight.

"My stars boy, what are you doing out there?" she asked.

"Ma'am, I am hungry, and I need a place to stay for the night. If you could just spare a little food, maybe a drink, I'd sure be beholden to you," I begged.

"Look at you boy, your shirt is torn, you have blood all over your face and you're dirty as a pig. What's your name and where are you from, boy?"

"Folks call me Rusty, Ma'am. I used to live up in Iowa."

"Well then, get in here Rusty. We need to get you cleaned up and get some food in your belly." She turned toward the inside of the building, "Ray, get out here, we've got company."

A big old man in bib overalls and a red flannel shirt limped up to the door. "What's goin' on here Miriam?"

"We have a visitor, Ray. I don't know where he came from or what he's doing here. He says his name is Rusty. The boy needs some help," she told him.

Ray pointed his cane at me, kind of mean like, and asked, "Whatcha doin' here, boy?"

I started to cry, and blurted, "My Momma died and they took my sister. There weren't no reason for me to stay on the farm no more."

I caught myself before I told him my whole story, but right away wished I hadn't told so much. I didn't say anything about the man in the truck though.

"Let's get you cleaned up. I'll heat up some leftovers. You can get your-self a good night's sleep, and then we can talk things out in the morning," she said. She smiled and took my arm to lead me in. "My name is Miri-am. That grumpy old fart with a heart of gold is my husband, Ray,."

I hesitated, but Ray looked at me sternly and ordered, "Get yourself inside here boy."

He brought me out an old pair of bibs, a clean shirt, and some socks. Miriam started some water on the stove for a bath and said, "You get out of those clothes. Here's a blanket. Wrap yourself up in it till I get the bathwater hot," she said, disappearing into the kitchen. In just a couple of minutes, she laid out a big bowl of stew, a huge chunk of bread, a hunk of cheese, and a big glass of milk.

"Fill your stomach before you get cleaned up. I'll fix the extra bed. You look plumb wore out," she went on.

I ate like I hadn't eaten in a week. Come to think of it, it had been over three days since I'd had a real meal.

After two bowls of stew–'bout the best I ever ate–and a bath, I crawled into the bed. And it was 'bout the softest bed I ever felt. I didn't toss and turn or anything and the next thing I knew, it was morning already. I woke up to the smell of fresh-baked bread and bacon frying in a skillet. Miriam had three places set at the table. Ray was nowhere in sight.

"You drink coffee, Rusty?" she asked.

"No, ma'am; don't like it much," I answered.

"Well try some anyway, son. It's good for you. It will make you feel all warm inside."

Ray came in, hung his hat on the rack, sat down, and asked again, "Whatcha doin' here, boy? Tell me the truth now. I need to know a lot more than you told us last night."

"Well sir, I'm goin' to visit my Grandma and Grandpa... I mean my un-cle."

"You're lyin' to me, boy. We don't stand no lyin' or half-truths here! Tell me the whole thing this time, boy, and it better be the truth."

"Well, sir, I used to live up in Iowa on a little farm with my Mama and little sister. My Daddy left when I was real little. Well, see, my Mama died. The government came and took my sister away. They was gonna take me too, but I run off. I don't have no kin nowhere and don't have no place to go or no place to stay."

"What'd ya stop here for?" he asked.

"Well, sir, I was tired and hungry. I lost my clothes and all my money. I didn't have nowhere else to go."

"We don't take in no boarders. It's just me and Miriam here and we like it thataway."

"Now Ray, be nice to the boy," Miriam scolded.

"I'm sorry sir, but I just don't have no place else to go," I said.

"We can keep the boy for a bit, Ray. It won't hurt anything. We can't just turn him out," she told him.

"If you're thinkin' on stayin' here you're gonna have to help out some; earn your keep," Ray grumbled at me.

"I wasn't plannin' to stay here, sir."

"Don't call me sir. My name's Ray, understand?"

"Yes sir, Mr. Ray."

"I ain't Mr. Ray. I'm just plain Ray."

He looked over at his wife, "Miriam, the boy is stayin' with us till he gets filled out some and knows where he's goin' next. From the looks of him, could take a while, but then he's movin' on."

He looked at me and repeated, "You're gonna have to help out here, boy. Do you know how to do anything?"

"Well sir, Ray, I can chore pretty good and garden some. I kinda have a knack for fixin' stuff too."

He said, "We'll get you goin' tomorrow. Till then, make yourself ta home," he turned and walked to the door.

"Don't let him worry you, Rusty, he's a good man. He just likes to scare folks a bit at the start. Don't worry, we are goin' get you back on your feet," she assured me.

They had a nice little store, Ray and Miriam; nothing fancy. They had some shelves of groceries on one side—canned goods mostly. The other side had some clothes, mostly work stuff, piled up on tables. There was some hats hanging on the wall above the clothes and a few pairs of work shoes lined up on the floor. Up front were some shovels and hoes and the like. There were a couple of tanks outside, one with kerosene and one with gas.

I was admiring a pair of work boots that looked to be about my size. "Them shoes are for sale boy," Ray said as he walked up behind me.

"I know. I don't have no money yet, but when I do, I'm gonna have me a pair. I've never had no new shoes before," I said.

"From the looks of you, they are gonna sit there for a while. We don't do much credit business. Come with me boy. We need to see about gettin' you started."

I followed him around the store to the back yard.

"Me and Miriam used to have a big garden here. Got to where it hurt our bones too much to work it. We had ta pretty much let it go. Since yer stayin' fer a while, I'm gonna let you work it back up. It's gonna need to be bigger, though. Used to feed the two of us, but now with you, there's three eatin'. Miriam'll get you all the seeds you need from the Earl May catalog. I like lots of potatoes and cabbage. Want some beans and corn, too. Anything more than that, you'll have to ask her. There's a shovel and hoe in the shed. The shed could stand some fixin' up, too."

"I'll have to fix the fence first, sir."

"I said to call me Ray. Tell you what—I'm gonna call you boy till you start callin' me Ray, then I'll call you Rusty. That a deal?"

"Yup, it's a deal, Ray. I am gonna have to fix the fence first before I do anything else. No sense planting anything if I can't keep the critters out."

"You'll find stuff in the shed. If ya need somethin' we ain't got, McDowell could have it down at the Livery," Ray said, then walked back around the house and out of sight, leaving me alone to figure everything out.

I spent the next several days fixing fence, hoeing weeds, and turning the soil. I found an old push-type cultivator with a broken handle and fixed it up. I fixed the hinges on the shed and patched the roof too. Miriam would bring me a glass of water every so often; sometimes a glass of tea, sometimes lemonade. I found a heavy wooden bench leaned up behind the shed. It didn't have legs, so I built new ones for it and set it in the corner of the garden so Miriam could sit and watch. Sometimes I'd see Ray watching me. He'd just smile and walk away when I saw him. He never said a word, though.

Once I got the garden all prepared, Miriam got me all the seeds and plants I needed. Once the seeds and plants were all in the ground, she came out with a bunch of flowers to plant.

"Will you please plant me a flower garden, Rusty? I've always wanted a flower garden. Ray just never seemed to find the time. Now he spends most of his day sitting in his chair on the front porch, visiting with anyone who stops by," she said.

I found some pictures on how to plant her flowers in the Earl May catalog and arranged the plants as best I could so they would be all around her bench. Neither one of them ever said any more about me leaving and I never said anything about it either. I liked it here, they treated me good, and I didn't have any place else to go. Besides, this was pretty close to Springfield and I still wanted to figure a way to get in there and find out about that orphanage place. When I wasn't working in the garden, Miriam had me inside helping in the store, putting stuff on shelves, setting stuff outside for display, and such. She kept a book with everything she sold and how much she charged for each item. At the end of each day, she figured it up so she'd know how much money she had and how much she could spend on more stuff to sell.

"I want you to learn how to keep my book, Rusty," she said one day. "You need to be able to keep track of the merchandise and money so I can leave you in charge sometimes."

"I never did learn numbers, Ma'am. They was hard for me and I didn't see no use for 'em neither," I mumbled.

"Well, you can read, can't you?" she asked.

"Not really, Ma'am. I just sorta look at the pictures and try to figure what's bein' said that way."

"We're going to fix that," she said. "Ray doesn't read and figure very well either. I never could get him to learn. He always said, 'I'm too old, I don't need no learnin' now,' but you're not too old and you're going to learn."

"I don't want to go to no school. The kids all know all that stuff better'n me."

"I won't send you to school. There would be too many questions for you to answer, about where you're from and all. I'll teach you here myself," she said.

I already knew it didn't do any good to argue with her. I'd seen her set Ray straight before, so I just shrugged.

From then on, every night, she'd spend about an hour with me. Sometimes it'd be going through some book line after line, learning each word and how to say it properly. Other nights, she'd sit with her store book, show me how to enter prices and stuff, then teach me what the numbers meant and how to use them to keep track. She taught me how to talk to customers when I worked in the store. I learned how to greet people like they were special like I had never seen them before. She said, "You should always say, 'May I help you?' never 'Can I help you?' Treat everyone as if they are special. It doesn't matter if they come in here often or it's their first time. Be courteous and friendly; make them think they are special because they are special. They came in here to spend hard-earned money, so we want them to like the experience. And if they don't speak well, that doesn't mean they aren't smart; it just means they didn't have the opportunity to learn."

Learning wasn't so bad. She would sit there and go over stuff as long as it took until I understood, and there weren't any kids there making fun of me. It wasn't long until it started becoming easier for me.

I began to read books. I liked to read; I didn't need to be told. Mrs. Wright, who had a store down in town had a bookshelf in her lobby. Before long, I read every book she had. It turned out that *The Adventures of Tom Sawyer* was my favorite.

"Rusty, come on out here and sit a spell," Ray called from the porch.

He was sitting in his chair out front, leaned back against the wall, chewing and spitting. I guess one of the reasons he spent so much time out here was because Miriam wouldn't let him chew in the house. I sat down on the stool beside him and leaned back, just as he did.

"We need to talk, son. You've been stayin' here what, two-three months? You never told us what you was doin' that first day you came here. You've been doin' real good, gardenin', helpin' and all. It's good that Miriam's been learnin' you how to read and figure. I think it's about time you told me about yerself. I know'd you was runnin', but you never told us what you was runnin' from or why," he said

I figured this day was coming but hoped it never would. I thought about what I should say and decided I should tell the truth since they both had been so good to me.

"I came from up in Iowa, Sir," and stopped.

He gave me that stern glare I had seen so often.

I started over, "I came from up in Iowa, Ray. My real name is Russell Jordan. Me, Mama, and my little sister Janie lived on a little farm north of Stockport. I hardly knew my Pa, he left in the middle of the night when I was about four. My Mama died and left me and Janie alone. We were doing fine, I was working the farm and working for a neighbor in his saw-mill. Janie and I were going to school most days until I couldn't go anymore because I needed to work more. I still walked Janie to school every morning and walked her home every night. The teacher asked Janie why I wasn't coming to school anymore, and she told the teacher that Mama died. Somebody found out we were alone down on the farm and a man and a woman came to take us away. They caught Janie and tried to grab me too, but I got away. They came back looking for me a couple of times but never could find me. Me and the neighbor went looking for Janie but couldn't find her. I couldn't stand living there alone anymore, wondering what they did with my sister. When we were looking for her, up in Fair-field, a lady in the sheriff's office there told me about some people stealing kids and selling them. She said she heard of a place down in Springfield, so I guess, when I ran away, I was sort of heading toward Springfield," I paused to catch my breath.

"How come you didn't tell me and Miriam about this from the git-go, son?" he asked.

"Well, at first, I was afraid to. I was worried you'd turn me in," I said.

"You know better'n that now," Ray said.

He reached out and put his hand on my shoulder. I looked up when he did, I could see his eyes were welling up with tears. I'd never seen him cry before. I didn't think he could.

"Yes, I know that now," I muttered.

"Well, then, how come you still never told us?" he answered.

"I guess I didn't know how to start with it."

We sat silently for the longest time. A couple of times, when I looked up, he was staring off, kind of blank, and tears were running down into his gray beard. Pretty soon, his chair creaked as he got up, "Just sit here a minute, Rusty. I need to go talk to Miriam."

I could hear them in the store, talking back and forth. I couldn't make out the words, but I could get the gist. Shortly, Miriam was sobbing, then it got quiet. Then they both came out onto the porch.

Miriam pulled me up off the stool and hugged me. She was squeezing me so tight I could hardly breathe. She was sobbing hard. Ray stepped up and put an arm around both of us. "Oh, Rusty, we had no idea," she cried. "You poor boy, I wish you'd told us."

Ray tried to break the mood, "Miriam's got a sister over in Springfield. She's gonna get ahold of her. Git her to see if that place is there. Git her to find out about it, if it is," he said.

Things were different after that. We didn't talk anymore about everything I told them that day. Ray put his hand on my shoulder every time he was close to me. Squeeze a little and smile. Miriam would look up and smile every time she saw me. Lots of times she'd start whimpering when she spoke. Ray would come out in the garden some days and help a little; hoe beans or some such. Some day's he'd even follow me into the workshop; ask me what I was fixing, who I was fixing it for. He'd never done that before. Miriam would stick her head out the window when I was working in the garden and ask if I needed anything. She'd sit quietly when we were doing my studies at night. Lots of times when I was reading out loud, I'd look up and she'd be sitting with her eyes shut.

Several uncomfortable weeks passed. Neither Ray nor Miriam said any more about what the sister in Springfield was doing. I couldn't concentrate well enough to work much in the workshop. I messed up the leg of a chair I was repairing and had to tell my customer it wasn't finished when he came to pick it up. I dropped a whole can of paint and spent most of an afternoon cleaning up the mess. I gave up my woodworking and spent my days in the garden. My mind was constantly spinning.

Is the orphanage stealing kids so's they can sell 'em? Is there any chance Janie will be there? Will anybody there even talk to us? Will we be able to look at records? Will I ever see Janie again?

Chapter 7

"*R*usty, we are going to close the store for a few days next week. You and I and Ray are going to ride the bus to Springfield Tuesday. I talked to Evelyn; she says there is an orphanage there. We'll see what we can find out," Miriam said.

Tuesday morning, I got up before dawn, dressed, and went to the garden to do my morning chores. I thought I could get everything done before breakfast and then have time to take a bath. My clothes were all packed, I'd done that last night. But this morning, there was a heavy dew, so I couldn't pick any beans. I got wet walking in the rows, brushing on the plants. Hoeing didn't work either, the ground was muddy, and I was making a mess. My shoes were covered, my pants legs were wet and dirty, and I had corn chaff sticking to me. I gave up. I was in the shed, trying to clean my shoes when Miriam called from the kitchen, "Breakfast, Rusty."

I hadn't even fed the chickens yet, breakfast was ready, and I still needed to bathe. "Calm down," Miriam said, "I know you're nervous, but today is going to be a good day, I just know it."

"But I still have to take a bath and we have to walk down to town and the bus gets here in less than two hours," I answered.

"It's going to be ok, we'll make it in time, Rusty," she assured me.

We could see Hidden Spring in the valley from the store. As we walked down the hill, I could see Mrs. Wright's café, where the bus stopped. I tripped several times and almost fell, watching for the bus and not watching for potholes in the gravel as I should. None of us spoke, Ray wasn't even humming his song, the one verse that he repeats constantly.

"See, I told you we had plenty of time," Miriam said. "You sit on the bench. I'm going inside to talk to Emma Wright. Give me a shout when you see the bus."

It was only a few minutes, but it seemed like hours before I heard the bus downshift as it approached a town. Ray called to Miriam, then we stood on the stoop, each holding our suitcase, waiting. "It's going to be few minutes folks, I've got a package for Mrs. Wright," the driver said, as he climbed from his seat and opened a storage compartment underneath. "You can put your bags in here after I get her package out."

We managed to stuff three bags into a space large enough for only two, then went back to the front of the bus to wait. The driver and Mrs. Wright acted like long-lost cousins, talking and laughing. Doesn't he know we are in a hurry?

"Ok folks, find a seat anywhere you like. We've got three more stops before Springfield, but we'll be there in no time," he smiled.

My feet were frozen to the ground. I couldn't step up. Part of me wanted to get on the bus, ride to Springfield, get Janie. Part of me worried she wouldn't be there, or we'd find out something terrible had happened to her, and part of me wanted to turn and run. Run forever, run from everything. Just run!

Ray took my arm with that old farmer's grasp of his and pushed me toward the step. He didn't say anything and I didn't resist.

The bus driver was wrong. It wasn't "no time"– it was a lot longer. At each of the three stops before Springfield, he got off and went inside. Each time we could see him in there laughing and talking to people. Is he driving too fast, so he'll have time to visit? Are we going to be late? Will Blanche still be waiting when we get there late? Am I going to find Janie?

"Here we are folks," he called from the driver's seat. I didn't realize Springfield was such a big city. It seemed like we took an hour just to get from the edge of town to the bus station. The bus slowed to a crawl when we got downtown. I saw cars and people everywhere. The bus ground to a stop at the first stop sign and more people than lived in all of Hidden Spring crossed in front of us. Eventually, our driver picked an opening, the bus lurched, and we went another block. We only traveled one block and had to stop at another sign; again, more people than lived in Hidden Spring crossed. As we crept closer to the center of town the buildings began to get bigger. Some were four or five layers tall. I asked Miriam, "Why do they have buildings so tall? Do they have ladders inside?"

"These are office buildings and hotels, Rusty. Big cities have lots of people living and working closely together."

"Why?" I asked.

"I guess I don't know the answer to that," she answered.

"It sure seems like a funny way to live," I said.

Our bus stopped, the driver got up and turned to the passengers. Please, no time for another visit, let's just stop for the passengers and get going again. "This is our last stop folks. Give me a minute to unload your baggage," he said.

I stood on the sidewalk, scared by all the people, and looked around. A huge sign "Bus Stop" hung on the front of the building. The building was a hotel, taller than any tree I had ever seen. It had windows, real glass windows, all the way to the top. People were going in and out the same door; it spun like a top when they walked through it. All the men dressed funny, like preachers. The women all wore strange shoes, like the ones the lady who took Janie wore.

"Blanche will be inside, Rusty. Bring your bag. Let's go meet her," Miriam said.

My feet were frozen to the ground again. I wanted to find Janie but didn't understand why going into this huge building was going to help. This time, Ray didn't grab my arm. He didn't look like he wanted to go in either.

"Come on, you two," Miriam called, as she started toward the spinning door.

It took me three tries to get through the door. It was harder than trying to get on the merry-go-round back at the school. The first two times, I chickened out at the last second; almost got my suitcase caught. Miriam and Ray were already through, watching me from inside when a nice lady took my hand and we jumped in together. She smiled at me when we got through, I said, "Thanks," as she walked away.

The ceiling was high. Great big fans hung down on long ropes. The room was bigger than the entire general store, bigger than the abandoned church across from it even. They had these big fancy lights way up on the walls, shaped like our kerosene lights, but they weren't kerosene.

47

Someone bumped me from behind.

"Move out of the way son, you're blocking the door," he said, kind of grumpy. Miriam took my hand and we started walking toward a fancy bench, covered with fancy material. It was like a rug was made to cover it. A lady sat there in a shiny blue dress and a big white hat. She stood up as we got closer. "Evelyn, this is Rusty, the young man I told you about. Rusty, this is my sister Evelyn," Miriam said. She shook my hand, dainty-like. She looked a lot like Miriam, but I hadn't seen Miriam all fancied up like Evelyn.

"Hi," was all I could think to say.

"Miriam told me you are looking for your sister. She said you think she might be at the orphanage here."

"I don't know, Ma'am, they took her, but I don't know for sure who they were or where they took her," I answered.

"Please, call me Evelyn, Rusty. We'll all go to the orphanage tomorrow and see what we can find out. Was this your first bus ride? Did you like it?"

"No Ma'am, not much. I mean, yes it was my first bus ride, but no, I didn't like it much. Can we go to the orphanage today, there's still some sunlight left?"

"They'll be closed by the time we can get there. You can spend the night at our house, then we'll all go out there in the morning," Evelyn answered.

Yes Ma'am." I said, but I was disappointed we couldn't go today. I wanted to get this over with.

Miriam and Evelyn started talking and laughing, I guess about old stuff, like things they did when they were kids. I stood uncomfortably, watching all the commotion in this huge room. Shortly, a long black car pulled up in front of the hotel. Evelyn said, "Good, there's James. We can all go to the house and relax. Miriam and I have a lot of catching up to do."

The door was still spinning, but in the other direction now. I made it through on my first try. Outside, the big black car sat next to the sidewalk. The driver got out, came around, and opened the back door, "Good afternoon, my name is James, I am Evelyn's husband. You must be Russell?" he said to me.

"Hi," I answered. "Yes sir, that's my name, but folks call me Rusty."

"Very good, Rusty it is," he answered, smiling. "We are glad to have you visit with us. Evelyn has told me about you and your sister. I hope we can help you tomorrow. But now, you look like a young man in need of a good meal, a nice warm bath, and a comfy bed. Let's get you out to the house, I'll bet it's been a long day. How about you ride in front with me and Evelyn; we'll show you part of town on our way to the house."

"Ok, sir," but I thought to myself–this man sure can talk. Evelyn held the door open for me and I slid in between them. I'd never been in a car like this before. It had all kinds of knobs and gadgets; it had a lever sticking out of the floor. James moved it every so often, the car would sound different, and then speed up or slow down. I wondered how long it would take to learn how to drive it. It was nicer than any car I had ever seen around Hidden Spring.

Springfield had a lot of houses all scrunched together. They were all were painted nice and had nice green grass in their yards. Most of the houses had cars parked alongside. Some even had garages with doors on the front. Doors that shut so you couldn't see inside.

James saw me looking at all the stuff inside his car. "It's a brand new 1933 Model 57 Buick Sedan, Rusty. The finest car made," he grinned, beaming with pride.

James turned off the road and pulled up to the side of a big white house. It had more than one level just like a lot of the buildings downtown. "Here we are," he beamed.

Evelyn led me up the front steps onto the porch while James put the car away. Their porch had a roof over it, just like Ray and Miriam's, but the wood floor was painted, and the two chairs were fancy. They had a nice table between them; not like Ray's old nail barrel.

"Why don't you and Ray have a seat?" Evelyn said. "I'll bring you both out a glass of tea and some cookies. James will be around in a minute. Miriam and I haven't talked in so long, we need to sit a spell."

"Tell me more about Janie," James said as he brought a chair from inside and sat with us.

I started at the beginning by telling about Mama, Janie, Mr. Webster, Moose, Pete, school, and everything. By the time I got to the part about those people coming for Janie and me, I was wiping tears off my cheeks with my sleeve.

"That's enough, Rusty," James said. "I didn't mean to upset you. I don't need to hear anymore. Maybe tomorrow, we can find something out for you." He turned to Ray, "Have you thought any more about moving to town to help me out? More folks are buying cars every day and once this depression thing is over, the gas business is going to take off. I've got two stations now and am thinking about building a third. After that, who knows? I sure could use your help."

"I'm sorry James, but Miriam and I kinda like it out there on the hill. 'Sides, the Standard Oil man is tryin' to get me to put in some new pumps. He says new ones'd make me top dog out there. Says that if'n I don't take 'em he's gonna have to let someone else. Says I'll be sorry if'n I don't. I'm getting too old for all this progress stuff, can't teach an old dog new tricks, ya know?" Ray said.

"Dinner is ready," Evelyn called from inside.

Once we sat, Evelyn prayed over the food, just like Miriam always did at home. She made a special request for God to help me find Janie. Nobody said much after that. There wasn't any more talk about Janie or Ray moving to town, just mostly James and Ray talking about the Buick and Miriam and Evelyn talking about growing up back somewhere in Illinois. They all seemed to know I had a lot of things to think about.

When dinner was done and the table was cleared off, Evelyn took me upstairs, ran me a bath, showed me where I'd sleep, and left me alone. Later, alone in bed, I couldn't think about anything but Janie, Mama, and back home until I finally fell asleep.

The smell of fresh biscuits baking woke me. At first, I thought I was back in Hidden Spring, but when I heard Miriam and Evelyn talking, I knew better. "Good morning Rusty, did you have a good sleep?" they said, almost together

"It was pretty good, I guess," I answered.

They both got quiet for a few minutes. They acted like they knew I didn't sleep much. Finally, Evelyn looked at me, smiled, and with a sense of regret, said, "James is gone to check on the stations. Once he gets back, we are all going to the orphanage."

I ate in a hurry. No one talked to me, which was good because I didn't have anything to say. As soon as I finished my plate and put it on the counter, I went out on the porch to be alone. Will she be there? That was all I could think about.

When I saw James and Ray drive up, I closed my eyes and leaned back in the chair, pretending to be asleep. They quietly walked past me and into the house.

It seemed like an hour passed before they all came out of the front door. "Are you ready?" Miriam asked.

I didn't answer, I was so scared I didn't know if I could even stand up, let alone walk. But when they all stepped down onto the walk, I rose and followed.

"We're all going in together, Rusty. I don't know what we'll find. We'll just ask if they have a little girl with blond curly hair or if they had one. We'll ask them to show us pictures of all the young girls they have for adoption. But we're not going to say anything about stealing children. Evelyn and I decided it won't do any good to make anybody mad. We are sure they won't help us if we make them mad, OK?" Miriam said.

I just nodded. I hoped they'd do all the talking, but if I had to, I knew I could, and I knew I would.

It was a big stone building. It looked like a school, only it had a big fence all around. Not a farm fence to keep horses and cows in–it was a lot taller and stronger, like to keep kids from getting out. Miriam and Evelyn held my hands as we climbed the big cement steps and walked up to the heavy door. The door was a big heavy thing, James had to push hard to get it to move. It scared me when it made a creaking sound as James pushed on it. Inside there was a big room with a tall ceiling. Fancy lights hung down from the ceiling, like those I'd seen at the bus stop hotel. There were some dark wooden chairs lined up against the wall by the door to sit on. Right in front of us was a big wooden desk that needed some fixing, with an older lady sitting behind it. She was fat and had gray hair and wore thick dark glasses. She had a white uniform and hat on like she was a nurse. But I didn't know why there would be a nurse here. She looked up, but didn't smile.

"Can I help you?" she said with a gruff voice.

Miriam and Evelyn stepped up. Miriam spoke, "Yes, we are looking for a young girl, about ten or eleven. She has blond curly hair and pretty blue eyes."

"I'm sorry ma'am, but if you want to adopt, you will have to fill out the proper paperwork, submit it, and have it approved by the state. Then you will be put on a waiting list. Even then, we can't guarantee the age or hair color of the adoptee," she frowned.

"Excuse me, I don't think I made myself clear," Miriam said. "We are looking for this young man's sister. She disappeared several months ago and we are trying to reunite the family."

"We are not at liberty to give out that kind of information, Ma'am. All adoption information is confidential."

"Is there someone else we could talk to?" Miriam asked.

"I can call the headmistress for you Ma'am, but I assure you she will tell you the same thing I have," she said, now becoming agitated.

"Please call her, we'll be glad to wait," Miriam said.

I watched as the fat lady struggled to get out of her chair and hobble off down the hall. She opened another large wooden door at the end and disappeared. We stood silently for a while until it became apparent that they were making us wait, probably hoping we would give up and leave. Evelyn said, "We may as well sit, this may take a while."

We sat in silence. At least fifteen minutes passed without anyone coming to see us. I hadn't expected this.

The door creaked and we all looked up to see a big woman with black hair, wearing a black skirt and white blouse and a dark blue fancy coat over the top walk in. She was followed by the nurse we had been talking to. They walked to the desk, where the nurse sat in her chair and the big woman stood over her. If the devil is a woman, this is what she would look like.

The nurse spoke, "This is Miss Raschid; she is the proprietor of our home."

"Nurse Fisher tells me you are looking for a little girl," the devil woman said.

Miriam stood, "Yes Ma'am. This young man has lost his sister. We were hoping to learn if she might have ended up here for adoption."

"I believe she told you that we do not divulge that type of information," Miss Raschid said, sternly.

"Yes, but we were hoping..." Miriam started.

The devil woman interrupted, "We are an adoption agency, not some lost and found facility. We are not allowed to give confidential information about any of our wards. We will not furnish a list of current or past adoptees, nor will we let you see photographs or tour our facility. Now, if there is nothing else," she growled, turned on her heel, and strutted back down the hall and through the door.

The nurse looked up from her seat, and with a grin mimicked Miss Raschid, "Now, if there is nothing else, you may leave."

Miriam stood for a moment, looking down at the lady, then turned and quietly said, "There is nothing more we can accomplish here."

Back at James' house, Evelyn silently fixed tea and cookies and we sat at the dinner table. James was the first to speak, "We can't let this end here. Ray and I will go to the courthouse to see what can be done. Rusty, don't give up hope. We still may be able to find your sister."

I didn't even look at him. I had hoped we would learn something today. I thought we might find Janie or at least learn if she was at the home, and if she wasn't, we'd know what happened to her. If she got adopted, they'd tell us where she went. Or they'd tell us she'd never been there. But I sure didn't expect them to be so mean.

After lunch, James backed out the Buick. He took me and Miriam and Evelyn back to the agency and let us out about a block down the street. "Walk around the place, look through the fence, see if anyone around the place will tell you anything. Ray and I are going on to the courthouse; we'll be back in a couple of hours and pick you up right here."

The fence started at the edge of the orphanage and enclosed an entire city block. The yard had a few swing sets and slides, but it wasn't fancy. The ground was almost entirely dirt, with only a few small trees inside. The kids were mostly standing around; no one was playing or laughing. Their clothes were all worn and most didn't fit. They all looked like they needed baths. It looked like a big prison for kids.

Evelyn said, "Let's just walk around, we can just look through the fence and not try to talk to anyone."

I walked slowly, looking at every kid I could see. It was hard to tell the girls from the boys; their hair was all about the same length and needed combed. Some were so dirty I couldn't tell what color hair they had. One by one, I checked them out, looking for anyone who resembled Janie. Miriam saw how upset I was and said, "If you tell me how tall you think she'll be, that might help."

"I don't know," I said. I now realized for the first time that I wasn't looking for a seven-year-old little girl anymore, and I didn't know how tall she'd be. After two trips around the block, we stopped to rest. As I stood in the shade clutching the fence, a small boy started walking toward me. He was smiling and I knew he wanted to talk, but before he could get to me, one of the women dressed in a uniform rushed over and grabbed his arm. "

You know you aren't supposed to talk to strangers," she barked, and dragged him away.

Miriam touched my shoulder and said, "I think we better move, Rusty. They don't like us standing here."

"Maybe this is the first recess and more kids will come out later. Can we walk around to the other side and look for a while?" I asked.

"OK," Miriam answered. I knew she was worried now.

I walked slowly, watching the broken sidewalk, and looking into the yard at the same time. On the far side, I stopped. There was a girl standing with three others who caught my attention.

"Look, there's Janie!" I exclaimed. "Let's get closer." I hurried until I was straight across from her, only the fence and about twenty feet separated us. I stepped up and put my face against it and stared.

In a few seconds, one of the other girls noticed me and said something to the group. They all turned and faced me. Her blond hair was stringy, darker than Janie's, and hung down over her face. She looked up with a mournful expression that didn't change when our eyes met. The girl didn't move. One of the others leaned and said something to her. She looked away.

"Is that her?" Miriam asked hopefully.

Before I could answer, Miss Raschid came hurrying out the door. She yelled something I couldn't understand to the girls. They all hung their heads and started sheepishly walking toward the door.

"No, that isn't her," I told Miriam.

"You people are not welcome here," Miss Raschid snarled. "If you don't leave here this instant, I will be forced to call the police."

"But we're not doing anything wrong," I pleaded. "We are just looking. I hoped I might see my sister."

"You must leave! Now!"

Miss Raschid turned to the two uniformed ladies in the yard and ordered, "Take all the children inside, this instant."

"Let's go, Rusty, there isn't any more we can do here," Evelyn said.

We walked back to the corner where James and Ray had left us. We sat on a bench to wait. Both Miriam and Evelyn tried to console me but I felt like this may have been my last chance to ever find my sister. Evelyn gave me her hankie for my tears. The sight of the black Buick approaching didn't help. Somehow, I knew it wasn't bringing good news.

Neither Ray nor James was smiling as the three of us got in the back seat. Mostly, I sat quietly between Miriam and Evelyn on the ride to the house. Each of them held my hands.

At the supper table, they began to tell me what happened. Ray and James had gone to the courthouse. First, at the sheriff's office, they were told that they had no complaints about the orphanage on file and the office doesn't have authority over adoptions. "Unless someone files a complaint and has evidence to substantiate, we have no reason to be on their property," the sheriff had told them.

They went to the county attorney and he told them that the state's guidelines don't require orphanages to keep public records. They found out that records kept by orphanages don't have to have the given names of children that enter the facility and the names they give the children and the families that adopt are not available to the public.

Evelyn said, "We're sorry Rusty, but there just isn't anything else we can do. But don't lose hope; someday, somewhere you will find her. Try to look on the bright side, somebody is going to take care of that cute little girl. Somebody will give her a good home. A girl like that will make out. You just have to have trust."

The next morning the five of us drove to the bus depot. Ray and I bought tickets and got on the bus for the trip back to Hidden Spring. Miriam was going to stay behind to spend time catching up with Evelyn. James shook my hand as I boarded. First Miriam and then Evelyn hugged me. Evelyn had tears when she squeezed me. "We are so sorry. We wish we could have found Janie. Please come visit us any time."

James's last words to Ray were about moving to Springfield. "I wish you would reconsider. I need help with the stations, and it would be so good to have you close. Miriam and Evelyn could see each other every day."

I looked out the window the entire ride.

I'll never see Janie again. I don't know where to look. She's gone.

Chapter 8

*E*arly that fall when the flowers started blooming, Miriam would be out there in the morning when I first came to care for the vegetables. She would sit there and talk to me until my work was done and stay long after I left. She'd read me a story or a poem and then tell me who wrote it and ask me what it meant. I liked being in the garden, working and listening to her while I worked. Time flew by, those days. I got to where the only times I thought about Janie was when I was in bed trying to go to sleep. I didn't know where to look or even how to look anymore. I thought about what Evelyn had said that day at the bus depot and hoped she was right, that Janie had a good family now and was happy. If I couldn't be with Janie, all I wanted for her was to be safe and happy.

Word got around that Ray had a new boy working for him and the kid was a handyman. It wasn't long before neighbors started bringing me things to fix. They brought chairs and tables mostly, some tools, and occasionally a big job like fixing a hay rack or a plow. I would find pictures of how things were supposed to be in the Sears catalog, then repaired what was broken or make a new part. Most times I did a pretty good job.

One morning, after chores, Ray came around with a big grin. Ray didn't grin much. "Come here son, I've got something to show you."

Just below the sign out front that read, "Ray and Miriam's Country Store, Hidden Spring, MO." hung a new board.

He had made a new sign, it read simply, "Rusty's Repair."

He put his hand on my shoulder and said, "What do you think, son?"

It was the first time he had ever shown any affection toward me since we came back from Springfield. It was the first time in a long time that I felt good. I got all misty-eyed. This was the happiest I had been since Janie.

Hidden Spring was a nice little town. Most of it lay in the hills on either side of a lake. Probably less than three hundred people were living there–mostly farm families and laborers who worked on the farms.

The water from the spring–the clearest water you can imagine–made a constantly flowing creek through the valley and formed the lake. The lake wasn't more than three acres–hardly big enough to be a lake–but the locals still called it a lake.

Our General Store overlooked the town below. The abandoned church across the street was the only other building up here. Many evenings I sat on the porch with Ray. He sat with his chair leaned against the wall whittling on a piece of wood and whistling that unrecognizable song, over and over. I would sit on the porch floor, leaned against one of the posts, and think. Sometimes I would look at the church and wonder. What happened? What prompted the members to abandon a church and build a new one so close by?

The farming around here was still done mostly with horses and mules. A few farmers had tractors, fewer still had a truck or a car. Ray sold gas to everyone who had a need, but he didn't sell much and not often. He was always out there though, on his porch, waiting for his next customer. He would sit out front for hours on his old chair, leaned back against the wall, whistling. I never did know what the song was supposed to be. He didn't whistle very much of it, but what he did, he did over and over. I often wondered if Miriam had banished him to the porch because of his incessant whistling.

That is how our days were spent; Ray on the porch, Miriam inside running the store, and me either in the garden or in my little repair shop.

Every day but Sunday.

Sundays the store was closed. So was Mr. McDowell's livery stable and Mrs. Wright's Boarding House and Cafe. Everyone went to church. Well almost everyone. Miriam went, but Ray never would. She tried to get me to go with her, but I just couldn't. Something about church had bothered Mama. I think she only took Janie and me because she thought there was something there we should have, but I never understood what or why. But after Mama died, I never went back.

Monday morning, Miriam was inside clearing up breakfast, Ray was in his chair on the porch, and I was fumbling with the door, trying to make it latch better when the Standard Oil man drove up.

"Hi Bob, come sit a spell," Ray said.

Bob went into his sales pitch again before he sat down, "How much gas you sell this week, Ray? Your tanks are about empty again. A full tank won't hardly last a week anymore. I can't get that delivery truck to stop more than once a week though. What are you gonna do when you run out? Tell your customers they have to go somewhere else? More and more folks are getting cars all the time. They're gonna need gas. Ya can't keep customers if you don't have gas. You're gonna have to get a bigger tank. I'm telling you, Ray, there's gonna be a lot more cars. Won't be long till everybody has one. You'll be sellin' more and more gas. Tthink of all the money you could be makin'."

Ray said, "I know, I know, but it's just gonna be too much bother."

"It won't be no bother at all if McDowell puts in a pump down at the bottom of the hill. No bother at all for you, cause then he'll get all the business and you can just sit here on yer chair, getting poorer. Look, Ray, here's a picture of what them new pumps look like. They'd look mighty nice sittin' out front here, don't ya think?"

"True enough, but they'd cost a lot, and these here I got are paid for," Ray said.

I'd heard all this back and forth before, so I wandered off toward the garden, leaving those two to banter.

I was bending over in the garden when I heard a voice. "What's your name, Mister?"

I looked up from picking beans and saw a boy about ten-years-old pressed up against the fence. His hands clasped the top wire and he kind of hung from it. He'd been hanging around watching me for a few days, but until now, he had never spoken. He was a skinny kid, with brown shaggy hair. He had on a pair of jeans that were too big for him. He had a long belt cinched so tight the end of it was hanging in front of him. He wore a tee-shirt with one sleeve torn and a rip in the bottom and an old baseball cap with the bill turned a little sideways. One tooth was missing from his smile, but his eyes showed me he was happy way down deep inside.

"I am not a mister. yet," I answered. "Folks call me Rusty. What's your name?"

He mimicked me, "I'm not a mister yet either. Folks call me Joey," he grinned.

"Well come around through the gate and talk to me, Joey."

Boy, that kid could talk! Mostly, he just asked questions. "What are you planting? Why so deep? How long before this gets ripe enough to pick? Where do you get the plants? How long does it take to get them?" On and on, endlessly. But he was a nice kid, and I liked having someone interested in what I was doing. It was nice getting to talk to someone who wasn't a grownup.

From that day on, Joey came around every afternoon at about the same time. He always stood hanging on the fence until I asked him to come in. Then he stayed until I was through working for the day.

Once the garden was all planted and weeded, I had time to work in my little repair shop. Joey continued to come every day and now would follow me into the shop. Always asking questions.

Little by little, I added to my tool collection. I made some myself, Mr. McDowell gave me a few things and I ordered some items from the Sears catalog.

The work in the shop fascinated Joey. Just like in the garden, he needed to know how each tool was used, where I got it, or why I had more than one. Oddly though, he only wanted to watch. He had no interest in learning to use any of them himself. He was always quick to offer a hand when I needed it but never took any initiative on his own.

He'd sit there on a little stool in his special place, smiling, talking, and helping when need be. He made my afternoons fly by.

One day, when I was in the garden pulling some carrots, he showed up at the usual time. But on this day, he had a small girl with him, holding his hand. She stood at the fence with him until I invited them both in. She wore a tattered gingham dress. I guessed it was probably the only one she had. And she had the prettiest, curlist yellow hair. She was shy though. She wouldn't look up, and she kind of hid behind Joey.

Joey smiled as he said, "This is my little sister. Her name is Mary."

"Hi, Mary. My name is Rusty." She looked down at her shoes, too shy to answer.

It was strange that Joey had never told me he had a sister, but I guess we never talked much about our families. I hadn't told him anything about Mama or Janie or Moose, so there wasn't any reason to think he would tell me about his.

Mary held fast to Joey's hand all the time they were there that day. She stood quietly and peeked up to watch me work. Every time I caught her looking, she quickly looked down again. Later, as they left, I caught her looking back several times. Each time, when our eyes met, she would look away.

This became routine. Every day Joey would show up with her in tow. Every day, she watched but didn't speak. Of course, it wasn't long before Miriam noticed our new visitor. "Who's your pretty little friend?" she asked.

"Her name is Mary; she is Joey's little sister. She seems nice but doesn't ever say anything. I don't know whether she can't talk, or she is just really shy."

The next day Miriam stood watching from the window and when Joey and Mary arrived, she brought out a pitcher of tea and four glasses. Miriam spread her favorite tablecloth, her fancy bright yellow one with the embroidered red and orange flowers around the edge. On the end of her bench, she set out the pitcher and glasses and some fresh muffins. "Why don't you kids come over here and have a glass of tea and a fresh muffin?" she called.

I leaned my hoe against the fence and motioned for Joey to come along. Mary followed silently, hiding behind Joey and holding his hand. Miriam gave us each a little plate with a steaming hot muffin oozing with butter and covered with jam. She set a big glass of tea at each place. We sat silently until we finished our snacks, then I saw Mary whisper to Joey and he immediately said, "We need to leave now."

Miriam and I watched them as they walked down the hill toward town. Joey turned back to look several times, but Mary didn't. Miriam was disappointed. "She's such a cute little thing, I hope she comes back," she said. "I hope I didn't scare her off. She seemed to like my muffins.

"Maybe that will be enough reason for her to come back. If your friend Joey keeps coming, maybe she might come too."

Both of us hoped we would get to see Mary again.

To my surprise, the next day, at the same time, the two of them were standing at the fence. I walked over, opened the gate, and let them in.

Once again, Mary didn't speak. Miriam watched from the window but didn't come out.

After a couple of days of this, Miriam tried again. This time she got Mary to sit on the bench with her when Joey and I went to the repair shop. I could see Miriam showing Mary the flowers, telling her all about them, but Mary only listened. It took a couple of days of this before she finally responded.

"I like your flowers," she said to Miriam.

That evening, after Joey and Mary were gone, Miriam was overjoyed. "I just knew she could talk. She's just really shy, but she's such a sweet little lady," she gushed.

In the weeks that followed, when they came through the gate, Mary went straight to the bench and waited for Miriam to come out with her bright yellow tablecloth with red, and pink, and orange flowers around the edges. Miriam would appear carrying tea or lemonade or water and muffins. Always muffins. The two of them were soon inseparable. Mary became interested in Miriam's flower garden and before long, she even took it over. Miriam would sit on the bench and watch as Mary pulled weeds, pruned leaves, and picked bouquets. Now, on most days, we had flowers for the dinner table and Mary always left with some in her arms. On those days when there weren't very many in bloom, it was Mary who always got the flowers. Miriam insisted. "Rusty, next year I want you to make my flower garden bigger," she said with a big smile.

One day Joey came by at the usual time but with Mary on one hand and an old kerosene lamp in the other. "Do you think you can fix my mom's lamp? It is our only light and she can't make it work."

This was the first time he had ever spoken of his family. In all the times we had talked I just assumed Joey and Mary had a mom and dad and lived somewhere in town. But most of the townspeople had electricity now, so maybe they lived in the country? Maybe they didn't have a mom *and* dad?

When I saw the dilapidated old lamp, it made me think of Mama. It stunned me to think how much Mary and Joey might be like Janie and me. Why hadn't I thought of this before?

"I've never fixed one before, but if you leave it, I will try to make it work again," I said.

Nothing could keep me from fixing that lamp. Joey didn't realize it, but we formed a bond that day. He couldn't have known that he went from a friend to a brother that day.

I got Mr. McDowell to teach me how to solder the hole in the bottom and I found a good chimney and wick in Mrs. Wright's junk pile. I had the lamp fixed and hanging on the fence post the next day when Joey and Mary came for their daily visit. He hugged me when I lit it for him. He watched it burn for a few moments, then started to cry.

I realized he didn't have any money to pay me.

That didn't make any difference to me. I wouldn't have let him pay for it anyway, even if he had money. He was embarrassed, and I couldn't convince him that I didn't care. "You're my friend, Joey. I can't take money from friends. I'm happy that I could figure out how to fix it," I said. Nothing I could say would bring that smile back. He grabbed Mary, who was already headed toward Miriam and the flower garden, took the lamp, and they hurried off.

"What was that all about, Rusty?" Miriam asked.

I explained to Miriam what had just happened and asked, "What should I do?"

"You will just have to let him work it out. Be patient, he'll be back," she assured me.

I didn't sleep, I spent the whole night worrying and hoping. How can something as simple as fixing an old lamp cause so much trouble? Aren't friends supposed to do things for friends? I'd be happy if Joey did something like that for me. I sure hoped Miriam was right, but I didn't think just being patient was going to work.

The next morning, I went to the garden early, worked all morning, and watched for Joey. I stayed longer than usual and every few minutes I looked toward the gate. But no Joey. Even Ray tried to ease my mind.

But nothing he or Miriam could say would make me feel better.

Next day was the same, I was in the garden early, earlier than the day before. I spent hours gazing at the gate. Still, no Joey.

I had never been to Joey's house, he never even told me where he lived, but I made my mind up to go find him the next morning. I couldn't let our friendship end this way. I wondered what Mary felt. How could she understand what happened?

I dreaded this morning. I picked at my breakfast until Miriam threatened to throw it out if I didn't finish it. I piddled around the garden until I was sure Joey and Mary weren't going to show. It took a long time to muster the courage, but shortly before noon I told Miriam, "I'm going down to the lake for a while."

"I baked muffins this morning. Why don't you take a few and a jug of tea just in case you want to stay for a while," Miriam said. She knew what I was intending.

I spent the afternoon talking to anyone and everyone I could find. Everybody knew who Joey and Mary were, but no one knew where they lived. I followed guesses and hunches until late afternoon, then walked back up the hill carrying an unopened sack of muffins. I had chores that needed to be done, but I would try again tomorrow. I was going to look every day for as long as it took.

Miriam saw I was still carrying the tea and the bag of muffins. "Ray and I did the chores, Rusty. Come in to dinner," she said.

The next morning I was sitting at the table picking at my breakfast, wondering what to do next. Miriam was standing in the kitchen looking out the back. "Rusty, come look out the window!"

Joey was standing at the garden gate with his back to the house.

I ran back to my room and threw on yesterday's clothes.

"Rusty, you know you are supposed to start every day with clean clothes. Today isn't any different. You get back in there and change, then go out there like this is just another day. Let Joey be the one to talk!"

But I burst through the door. No way could I act like this was just another day.

Joey turned and he was already crying. I was too. "Rusty, I'm sorry I can't pay for the lamp."

"I won't let you pay for it. I fixed the lamp for you. I wanted to do it. Let's never talk about this again, deal?"

"It's a deal!" he answered.

Mary came with him the next morning and every morning after.

For a long time now, I had been looking at Ray's chair–the one out front that leaned against the wall. He spent a lot of time in that chair. It probably was a nice chair once, but not anymore. Two of the back slats were missing and a third was broken. He had fixed one arm by wrapping twine around it. Several attempts at repair had been made over the years but hadn't been successful. I decided to make a new one for him.

I wanted it to be a surprise, which wasn't easy since he was always around. I got some red oak from Mr. Hickenbottom, who had a small sawmill behind his barn. His wasn't nearly as nice as Mr. Webster's back home but it would make a good chair. It made me think of Mr. Webster. I knew he would be proud of the way I was getting on, especially since now I was doing so much woodwork. To keep Ray from suspecting, every time I went down to town, I would pick a few pieces and carry them back in my bag. I had to stash them in the ditch close to the General Store and go get them when Ray wasn't looking. I kept the chair under an old blanket in the corner of the shed. As the chair progressed, the blanket got taller. Ray noticed it and a couple of times asked me what was under the blanket. I told him it was just some wood I was saving. That wasn't a lie, but it wasn't the truth either. I hated lying and I didn't want to get caught in one by either Ray or Miriam.

I asked Joey if he could come early one morning to help me. So, while Ray was helping Miriam inside, Joey and I quickly replaced the old chair with my new one. Then we hid in the bushes to watch. We told Miriam about it ahead of time. So, once she knew we were done, she sent him out to get the mail.

Ray walked out the front door, stopped to look around like he always did. He stood there for a minute, kind of taking in the new day. As he stepped off the porch, the new chair caught his eye.

He hesitated in mid-step, stumbled, and almost fell. Joey and I had our hands over our mouths trying to keep from laughing.

He stepped back on the porch, looked around to see if anyone was watching, then moved to the chair, stopped, and looked around again. Still didn't see anyone. He picked the chair up and kind of twirled it around on one leg as he checked it out. Then he set it back down, leaned it against the wall, stepped back to look at it, and grinned. He stood the chair back on all four feet, sat in it, and leaned back. He closed his eyes and just leaned for a bit.

"You can come out now. I know you're watching," he said.

Joey and I burst from the bushes. In the same instant, Miriam was on the porch.

"Nice chair. I wonder who made it?"

"I made it, sir, and Joey helped me."

"I've been thinking I needed a new one," he smiled, then repeated, "Nice chair. I believe I'll set me a spell; see how it fits."

After that, if he was outside and wasn't busy, he was in his new chair.

He never said any more about me hiding it. Never let on that he knew what was under the blanket. Never asked about the old chair. Never asked where I got the wood. Nothing like that. But he sure liked that chair. Every time someone new came on that porch, he would show it off. He made everyone sit in it, pointed out how comfortable it was. And every time he'd say, "Ain't this about the bestest chair you ever seen? Rusty built me that chair!"

I was glad he liked it. Made me proud. Made me think I could fix most anything.

Chapter 9

*M*ary came around alone one day. She hadn't come alone before, and she was earlier than normal. I was picking beans when she arrived. She was carrying an old music instrument case under her arm. "Joey's sick today, sneezin' and such. Is it ok if I sit in the flower garden?"

"Sure, I'll get Miriam."

"It's ok, I don't mind being alone." She walked over to the bench and sat down amongst the flowers.

She'd never come alone before, so as soon as I got a basket full of beans picked, I went over and sat beside her. "What's in that case?" I asked.

"It's just an old mandolin. My momma has had it forever. It sits in the corner by her bed. I'd like to learn to play it. Can you fix it for me?"

"I'll try. Let me see it." She handed me the old beat-up thing with only two strings. The neck was cracked and one of the adjusting knobs was gone. After I looked at it, I wished I hadn't said I'd try. But she had the most sorrowful look on her face.

"This might take a while," I told her.

"That's okay," she smiled.

I asked Miriam about it, but she didn't know anything about music or instruments.

"Why don't you ask Mrs. Wright?"

I wrapped it in an old towel and down the hill I went.

"Sorry, Rusty, I don't play music. Mrs. Morrison plays the piano in the church. She might know something about mandolins. She lives out on Hackberry Lane. Yyou might ask her."

I walked to the end of Hackberry and back. Then I went back again but couldn't find her house. I was standing in the street, about to give up, when I heard church music coming from behind a stand of cedar trees.

There was a lane through the trees I hadn't noticed, so I walked through to see where the music was coming from. Past the grove of cedars, I saw a big old two-story house with three cars and an old horse and buggy sitting out front. The music was coming from inside.

I stood on the porch, listening, and wondering for a bit, then knocked. The door opened and a tall lady with gray hair and long fingers stood in front of me. "Yes?" she asked.

"Howdy Ma'am, my name is Rusty. I live up on top of the hill at Ray and Miriam's General Store. I was wondering if you might help me with this mandolin. It belongs to a friend of mine. I'd like to fix it up so she could learn to play it. Mrs. Wright sent me. She thought you might be able to help me," I blurted.

"Come in young man, my name is Mable Morrison. I don't play anything but piano and organ. I have some friends inside. Maybe one of them might be able to help. We'll see what we can do," she said.

A big black shiny piano sat on a fancy round rug in the middle of the living room. Four ladies and one man sat in chairs next to it. There were a bunch of paintings on the walls–pictures of waterfalls and mountains; stuff like that. A fancy light with lots of little lights hung right above the piano. It hung down a long way from a high ceiling.

"These are my friends. They are in our church choir," she said. "Now, let's see what we can do."

She rummaged through some papers and found pictures of people playing mandolins, but not much else. "Sorry, Rusty. I don't seem to have anything that can help you. Next time we have choir practice, I'll ask Howard Pratt to come by. He plays violin and I think maybe mandolin too. Come around next week at the same time, and we'll talk to him about it."

I went home disappointed, but not discouraged, then got out the Sears and Roebuck to see if that would help. They had mandolins for sale in there, but no parts and no music. I would have to wait on Mrs. Morrison and Mr. Pratt.

The next morning, I was sitting on the stoop pondering what to do next and found myself staring at the old church across the road. I wonder what's in there.

The door was cracked open, but it was stuck. I went back to my shed to fetch a pry-bar to force it open. Even with the bar, it was hard to move. I had to pry up on the bottom and push with my shoulder.

I didn't feel comfortable when I stepped inside. It felt like someone was in there with me. It was eerie. All the pictures had been taken. I could see by the light spots on the bare walls where they once had hung. I walked around looking, but didn't know what for. The pews were all still there; a few even had songbooks on them. I sat in one. The room was hazy, I guess from the dust I had stirred up. The light made streaks in the dirty air. One streak hit the podium where the preacher used to stand. I wondered what it had been like in here on Sundays when the pews were full of people and the preacher was up there preaching and the choir was up there singing.

Still, I felt the eerie presence. I thought I heard footsteps, then felt someone sit beside me, but when I looked, I was still alone. While I was looking away, the sun went behind a cloud and when I looked back to the front, the streak of light was gone. It was like the preacher was done and everybody had gone home.

I closed the door behind me as best I could.

Miriam stuck her head out the back door, "Rusty, there is a Mr. Pratt here to see you."

I laid down my hoe and came running to the house.

"Hi Rusty, my name is Howard Pratt. Mabel Morrison asked me to stop by. I understand you want some information on mandolins," he smiled.

I followed him out to his car where he opened the back door to a stack of sheet music and four or five mandolins. A couple of them needed repair.

"I don't play anymore but I would be glad to help you fix the one you have and get you started on how to play."

"It's not for me. I have a friend who wants me to fix her mother's so she can play it," I said.

We spent the afternoon talking about everything he knew about music and mandolins. I didn't understand most of it, but he was so enthused with the prospect of helping someone learn that the time just flew by.

Miriam finally interrupted us to say supper was ready and asked Mr. Pratt if he would join us. He said he couldn't, but left me with two mandolins for parts and a bunch of information on how to repair Mary's.

For the next week, I spent every spare minute working on Mary's instrument. Two days later, Mr. Pratt came back with a bridge, new strings and a nice piece of rosewood to make a pickguard from. We talked some more about how to repair it and about some issues I would encounter. I told him about Mary and that I was fixing it for her. When he heard that, he said, "I'd be glad to give her lessons if you'd like."

"That would be great, but she can't afford to pay, so I'll pay for her," I said.

"I meant I will give her lessons, Rusty. These old hands don't let me play anymore. It will be nice just to hear mandolin music again," he said smiling at me.

Within the week the mandolin was fixed. I asked Mr. Pratt if he could come around early some morning so I could give it to her and introduce him.

Two days later, I had it all set up. Mr. Pratt was at Miriam's table drinking coffee and I was working in the shed waiting for Joey and Mary to come. When they got here, Mary went straight to the bench and sat waiting for Miriam. I took Joey with me to the shed, showed him the mandolin, then put it back in the case, and asked him to lag behind me and carry it for me.

It was such a beautiful morning. The sun was glowing through the puffy white clouds. The air was fresh from last night's rain. It was the perfect time to show her.

Miriam and Mr. Pratt were peeking out the window. Ray had come and was watching from the corner of the house. Mary walked over to the bench and sat waiting for Miriam to come out like she always did. Joey tagged along behind me as I walked up. Then, after I sat beside Mary, he came up with the mandolin case wrapped in paper under his arm. My eyes were already burning from the tears that were forming.

My words came hard as he laid the package on the bench next to her. "Mary, I have something for you," I said.

Her fingers gingerly tore back the wrapping and opened the case. She paused to look before lifting it out.

"Oh, Rusty, it looks so wonderful. I'm so happy." She held it up for all to see. "See my mandolin. Rusty fixed it for me."

Tears were streaming down her face. "I can never thank you enough."

"Please, just learn to play it," I sobbed.

"I will. I will. I promise. I promise I will!"

She hugged me for the longest time. It was the best hug I had felt in a long, long time.

"Mary, this is Mr. Pratt. He used to play the mandolin. He helped me a lot when I was fixing yours. He even gave me some of the pieces I needed. And, if you like, he would be glad to give you lessons."

"Oh, that would be wonderful," she grinned.

But she just sat on the bench hugging that mandolin. Finally, she plucked the strings. Mr. Pratt positioned her left hand on the strings and showed her which string to pluck with her right hand. I don't know what note she played, but it was the sweetest sound I ever heard. She played that same note time and time again; and each time she looked up and grinned. "I can't wait to show my mama," she said.

I watched as she skipped down the hill, Joey and Mr. Pratt in tow, trying to keep up. I wished I could have been there to see the look on her mother's face.

I never saw Mary without her mandolin after that. At first, she would sit on the bench with Miriam and clutch it to her chest. Gradually she began to learn and would play something new for us every day. She amazed me by how fast she learned. The music she made with it was so sweet.

Chapter 10

Joey got an afternoon job at Mr. McDowell's livery. It kept him so busy that he couldn't come by every day. Our visits became fewer and fewer. When he did come, he couldn't stay very long. Sometimes he came directly from work. When he did, Mary didn't get to come with him. More and more I felt alone. I missed seeing them every day. I spent my time in the garden, doing chores and working at my repair job but somehow it wasn't enough. I found myself sitting in the shed or on the front porch. My mind wandered. I was lonesome. I thought about my first day here and what Ray had said. "Miriam, the boy is stayin' with us till he gets filled out some and knows where he's goin' next."

Maybe it was time to leave.

That night at supper, I couldn't eat. Miriam had made my favorite, fried chicken, but I just picked at it. I hadn't said a word throughout the whole meal.

Miriam broke the ice, "Something's ailing you Rusty, what is it?"

"I've been thinking. Maybe it's time for me to move on. I remember when I first came here, you told me I could stay till I got on my feet. Well, I've been on my feet for a long time now. I think it's time for me to leave," I said.

She started to answer, but Ray lifted his hand to shush her and said, "Rusty, this is your home, you belong here. You're the son we never had. We want you to stay. We want you to stay forever. We won't stop you from leavin' if you think you need to go, but more than anything, we want you right here forever!"

I opened my mouth to answer, but no words came out. For a few uncomfortable moments, we all just sat there. Then Miriam got up and began to clear the table. Ray went out the front door. I knew he was sitting in his chair. Miriam squeezed my arm as she picked up my plate and silverware.

I spent the night huddled in a corner of my shed.

When I woke the next morning, the sun was shining through the window. It took me the longest time to muster the courage to go to the house for breakfast.

The table was set. Ray and Miriam were in their usual chairs. Neither had eaten anything yet. Neither looked up.

I sat down in my spot and reached for the biscuits. Miriam reached out and took my hand, "Rusty, let's pray before we eat." She never prayed at a meal before. Ray didn't like her to. But today we all three bowed our heads.

We never talked about my leaving again. I sensed they thought about it often; but in truth, the only time it crossed my mind was when we sat down to eat. It was always uncomfortable. I knew Miriam wanted to pray and Ray didn't want her to.

Two strange men drove up to the gas pumps one afternoon. Ray pushed his chair away from the wall, rose, and stepped off the porch to greet them, "You boys need some gas?" he asked.

"I'll take five gallons," one answered.

"I never seen you boys around here before," Ray said.

"We work for the highway. The state is going to move the road. Instead of coming down the hill into town then, back up the other side, they're going to build a bypass. The new road is going to stay up here on top of the ridge and circle around to the hill on the far side. We are out here finishing up the plans and plotting it out," he answered. "You got anything to eat in there?"

"We don't sell food. We have some sodas in the cooler. I think we could rustle up some cold chicken and some beans if you like. There might be some cornbread left over too," he told them.

"That would be great for today. But I'm asking about every day. See, there's about a dozen of us on the crew. We are going to be here for quite a while. It sure would be nice to have a place to eat lunch every day."

Miriam fixed them a quick lunch and we all sat on the porch and talked. They said they would be here for about a month. They said if we wanted to fix up a little eating spot inside, he'd make sure they came every day until their work was finished. "We'll make it worth your time," he said.

It seemed like a good idea to us. I could fix up a long table and make a bench easily. The garden was kind of slow right now so I could help Miriam with the food. Miriam admitted, "We could use a little extra money."

It turned out to be a lot more work than she imagined. Every day twelve to fifteen hungry workers showed up all at one time. They were all starved, all wanted to eat at the same time, and all of them were in a hurry. I spent a couple of hours helping Miriam get the food fixed. Then we had the wild scramble of trying to feed everyone all at once. Even Ray pitched in a little.

Joey and Mary weren't coming around as much now, so I was lonely and needed something else to fill my time. Word spread about us "opening a café," so some of the locals and passers-by began to stop in, wanting to eat. I built another bench and a long table and set it out on the porch because we didn't have any more room inside. Every day, we had a line of folks waiting for a seat. Before long we were serving from about 11:30 to well after 1:00. Miriam didn't have a big enough kitchen to prepare all that food.Soon the wild scramble every day got to be too much for us. A month passed but still, they came.

"Two more weeks," they said. But two more weeks passed. Then they said, "Two more weeks; we promise."

Exhausted, Miriam put a sign on the door that said we were going to close our lunch business, but they continued to come, and she couldn't turn them away. We heard a lot of grumbling. People had come to count on eating at the store. Miriam's food was great, but it was just too much work for her. Evenings she was so tired, she laid on the couch while I cleaned up the dinner tables. Mornings, she slept late. Soon the General Store began to struggle. Customers had to wait while she looked for their orders. Inventory didn't get replenished. Special orders from Springfield didn't arrive as she promised. The new workers were still here and now wanted to buy gas and snacks. Ray broke down and bought the new pumps and bigger tanks that the Standard Oil Man had been pushing. He was working a lot harder than he wanted to.

Miriam became ill. She was tired all the time. Sometimes she had a fever and sat in her chair or lay on the couch.

We closed the lunch counter. That eased her burden, but she didn't recuperate. She spent most days in her chair unless a customer came in. Evenings she lay on the couch until bedtime. It was obvious she was more than just tired. The following week she got worse. She couldn't get out of bed one morning. But she kept denying how sick she was.

"Just give me a couple of more days; I'll be as good as new," she'd say. But a couple of more days didn't help. If anything, she got worse. We insisted she go to the doctor.

Ray looked down at her bed and sternly told her, "Tomorrow morning, we're goin' to Springfield." Ray didn't talk like that to Miriam often and when he did, she would get her dander up and talk back to him. Today, she just nodded her head.

Ray and I helped her to the car. I watched quietly as they left for the trip to Springfield.

Tears began to blur my vision as I watched the car disappear. They'll just be gone for a day, I told myself.

Night came and they hadn't returned. Another day, and I still hadn't seen or heard from them. On the third evening, Mrs. Wright's maid climbed the hill. I watched as she walked, head down, slowly. Every step seemed to be taken with effort. I feared the news she was bringing. "The delivery man brought a note from Ray this afternoon. He said to tell you that Miriam is sick. They say she has pneumonia. He said he is going to stay in Springfield until they know more. He said he wants you to stay here and run the store. He said he knows you can. He said to try not to worry," she said.

Then, she wiped the tears from her eyes and put her hand on my shoulder. "The church is all praying for Miriam and Ray. We will pray for you too, Rusty. Please, if you need anything, let us know," she murmured.

I thanked her and watched as she walked to the bottom of the hill and disappeared into the boarding house. Thoughts bombarded my head that evening. I sat on the stoop until way after dark. I hadn't felt this empty since I left the farm six years ago. I spent the night laying on the bed staring into the dark, wondering what it all meant.

I thought about Miriam. I thought about Mama. I thought about Janie. Why do good people have to suffer?

A ray of light shot through the window. A new day meant I would at least have things to do. Things to occupy my mind. Things that could help me cope.

I fixed eggs and biscuits but couldn't eat them. I opened the store, but no one came. I was sure the word had spread in town. No one knew whether we were open and those who needed something were staying away. I spent the day cleaning and organizing shelves. I caught up with the books and filled some orders. In the afternoon I went to the garden and tried to work but even hoeing weeds wouldn't dull my mind. I wished Joey and Mary would come to visit.

Days dragged by without receiving any more news. A week; still nothing. Little by little customers began to come back in. I was uncomfortable when they wanted to know if I had any news and I didn't. That made me even more depressed. I put a sign on the window, "Knock if you need anything." I turned off the lights and kept the door closed.

From the garden one day I saw Mrs. Wright climbing the hill. Her maid was holding her arm, helping her walk. I could see they both had red eyes. I knew they were bringing bad news.

They stood in front of me, each holding the other's hand. Mrs. Wright finally spoke, "Rusty, Ray said Miriam won't live very much longer. He said he is going to stay in Springfield until she passes. He said he is not ever coming back here. He said he is going to live with James and Evelyn and help James with his business. He said he wants you to have the store. He will have Mr. Walker take care of the legal stuff, transferring the deed and all. He said to tell you he is sorry it has to be this way, but he just can't bear the thought of being in the store without Miriam. He said he will miss you. He said he will maybe come to see you someday. He said James and Evelyn said you are welcome there any time for as long as you want to stay. He said he loves you like a son. He said he misses you every day and always will!"

We all three stood, nobody saying anything, just hanging our heads.

Mrs. Wright finally broke the silence, "I'm so sorry, Rusty." She and her maid both hugged me tight and turned away.

My tears made it hard to focus as they left me standing in front of the store, alone.

I wiped my face with my sleeve, closed the door, turned out the lights, and spent the night in my shop.

Chapter 11

I never opened the store again. I knew why Ray said he couldn't bear to come back here. I knew he was feeling empty and alone. I felt empty and alone too. I knew the feeling would never go away. I spent my days tinkering, walking in the woods, and sitting in the garden. I walked across the road to the abandoned church. I imagined the church felt just like me, alone and abandoned. I went in a couple of times but whatever I saw in there before was gone now. I spent my evenings lying in bed, staring at the ceiling. I found myself standing in front of the store, looking at all the memories–the signs hanging under the porch, Miriam's bench and table, Ray's chair. I couldn't bring myself to sit in either one of them. I quit bathing. I didn't shave for the first time. My beard was red, which made me think of Grandpa Red. Joey and Mary came but I couldn't talk to them. Mary would sit on the bench with her mandolin, but she wouldn't play. Joey watched me from the fence, but I didn't invite him in.

Mrs. Wright's maid came alone one day carrying an envelope. Mr. Walker's name was on the outside. I opened it. Inside I found the deed to the property signed over to me by Ray. I put the deed back in the envelope and put it in the desk drawer.

I knew I was going to leave.

I offered the store first to Mr. McDowell, then to Mrs. Wright. Neither wanted to buy it. I bought two new padlocks and returned home. I went into the store for the first time in several days and got a new pair of boots, my clothes and all the food I could carry. I got my can of money from under my bed, counted it, and divided it into three equal amounts. I put each pile in a separate envelope. I put one envelope in my pack and addressed the other two. I wrote Joey's name on one and Mary's on the other.

I took two more envelopes and addressed one to Mrs. Wright and put a note leaving the store's inventory to her; the other to Mr. McDowell with a note telling him I left the contents of my shop to him. Then I waited for nightfall.

Once the sun had set, I walked down the hill to town.

I sat on the bench at the edge of the lake for a while until I felt ready, then I went to the cafe. I gave the four envelopes to Mrs. Wright and asked her to see that they were delivered, thanked her, and turned away before she could speak.

The moon was up now and almost full.

I walked all night.

The days and nights on the road did nothing to ease my pain. The hours spent alone made the loneliness worse. I didn't know where I was going, only that I needed a new life. I couldn't go back to either of the ones I left behind.

This road of endless hills didn't help, sometimes it would take an hour to get to the crest of one only to see another and another in the distance. Some folks would stop and offer a ride. Sometimes I accepted. Most times I didn't. When they asked, "Where ya goin' boy," I didn't have an answer.

One day, somewhere in Arkansas, I stopped to watch a bunch of men putting up hay. They noticed me after a while and the one who was bossing the rest of them came over to the fence. "You want a job boy? We sure could use another hand."

He seemed nice enough and I didn't have any place to be, so I accepted the offer. "We're gonna be here about two weeks before we move on. You can go with us if you like." I told him I'd stay till they were done, then I would move on.

It was hard work. It was hot. This wasn't something I wanted to do for very long, so when the last of the hay was up, the boss came around to settle up and I told him I'd be leaving in the morning. I spent that last night helping them load their rigs and pack away equipment. "We'll be leavin' first light; sure you don't want to come along?" he asked.

"No, I'm going to keep moving south," I answered.

That last day, when they were done, someone opened a bottle of whiskey and they began to drink. I didn't want to be a part of that, so I moved off a little, spread my blanket, and fell asleep.

The warm morning sun hit my face and slowly brought me awake. I didn't smell coffee; the men were gone. I rolled over and looked around, there wasn't a soul in sight. They had left before sunrise.

I tied my bedroll to my pack then reached under my hat for my boots.

They were gone. An old worn-out pair lay in their place.

I saw my pack wasn't tied. I opened it up, stuck my hand into my money hiding spot. It was empty. My money was gone too.

All they left was my pack. At least my food bag was still hanging in the tree where I kept it.

Now alone, lonelier than ever, broke, and with a broken-down pair of boots without laces, I still had no good reason to turn back. I walked on south.

It was hot today. About the hottest day I'd ever seen. My feet were getting sore from the boots. I walked through a little town named Marked Tree. It was in the hills when I walked into town and when I walked out, the hills were gone. The land was flat for as far as I could see. I'd never seen anything like it—flat as a tabletop. I sat down, leaned up against a big oak tree to ponder what to do. I took my bottle out and drank almost the last of my water. I was thinking I should go back into town and fill my bottle before I went on.

"Where you headed? You need a ride, son?" a nice old man asked from the cab of his pickup. He had a woman in there with him.

"I need to fill my water jug first."

"Hop in, I've got water. We're headed to Memphis. You goin' that way?"

"Memphis is as good as any," I answered and crawled in.

"Them sure ain't much in the way of boots you got there," he smiled.

"I was haying with a crew a way back. They moved out in the middle of the night. One of them stole my boots and my money while I was asleep."

"I ain't got no boots fer ya, but I got a brother down in Memphis. He works a crew on the river. He's always lookin' fer 'nother hand; I'll drop you off there if ya want. He'll put ya to work."

That old man and his wife talked nonstop. I answered all his questions about me, giving them as little true information as possible. Mostly, they talked about themselves. By the time we pulled into Memphis, I knew all about him, his family, their farm, and a lot of other stuff that was of no interest to me. For the first time in days, I forgot about being lonely.

"His name's Larry; tell him brother Bob sent you. Tell him I said to sell you a pair of boots. He'll let you make payments, but he's gonna charge you interest. Tell him brother Bob says, 'Hi'," he said as I climbed out and watched as them drive away.

I had never seen anything like this. A big wooden dock lined the river-bank; it had to be over a block long and wider than our yard and garden and the woods next to our store back in Hidden Spring. Everything you could imagine was lined up on the dock. There were bales of cotton, hay, wheat, and rice in rows. Rows of big boxes sat next to the bales. A mountain of corn was piled on the far end of the dock. Men were working all around; some were loading barges, others unloading. There was a line of big trucks waiting to have cargo loaded or unloaded. Some of the men were white and some black. I had never seen a black man before.

I asked a man who I thought might be in charge where the office was. He scowled and pointed at a little shack down on the bank. The sign above the shed door read "office." The dilapidated door screeched when I pushed on it.

"I need some work. A man gave me a ride here. He told me to tell you that brother Bob sent me and you would give me a job," I said.

"So, brother Bob sent you, huh? Well, that don't mean as much to me as he thinks it do. What's yer name boy?" Larry asked.

"Folks call me Rusty," I answered.

"Where ya from Rusty?" he asked.

"I'm from Iowa, sir."

"Iowa–that's up north somewhere ain't it? Up there in Yankee country?" Larry sneered.

"Yes, it's up north," I said.

He turned to four men who were standing off in a corner talking among themselves. "Well looky here boys, we got us a Yankee Boy."

I didn't like the tone of his voice. He sure wasn't anything like his brother, but I needed a job, so I didn't say any more. Right away I knew I wasn't going to like it here.

He took me down to a barge and yelled, "Hey, boys, all ya'll's gonna git to work with a genuine Yankee Boy!"

He put me up in a boarding house next to the dock with all the other white men. The black men lived in a row of shacks a block away. The blacks and whites tolerated each other, but neither had much to do with the other. Every morning we lined up and waited for it to get light enough to work. Bob, who told me to call him "Boss Man," gave out job assignments. Then we all worked until it was dusk every evening.

They had some big cranes that picked up the bundles and either set them in barges or took them out to the line of trucks, depending on whether they were being loaded or unloaded. There were some tractors and smaller trucks for moving stuff around, and each had an operator assigned to it. The new guys like me and all the blacks worked on the dock hooking, unhooking, shoveling, pushing and pulling. There wasn't much thinking done on this job. Just always some guy shouting orders.

Every night the white guys got drunk. They sat on their bunks and played cards or dice and passed a bottle around. I had never seen any of this and didn't know how to play but wasn't about to learn how anyway. Come payday they all tried to get me in their games, knowing they would clean me out. It used to get bad in there at night once they got drunk. Then they always began to fuss and fight. There seemed to be two groups in my house that didn't like each other for some reason. One would start something with a guy from the other group and in no time they'd all be fighting. Sometimes somebody would get stabbed or beat up with a club. They were always trying to get me into their fights; get me to join one side or the other. I didn't want any part of it, so after dinner was over I would go back to the river.

Several of the black guys would be down there fishing, shooting dice and playing cards. Sometimes they would get into an argument, but never like the guys back at the boarding house. They seemed to feel bad for the way I got treated by all the white guys. I hated being called "Yankee Boy," although I didn't understand why it was bad.

Down at the river, they all called me Rusty. I fit in better with them than my roommates.

Two of the black guys took a liking to me. I'd sit by them and talk while they fished. Their names were William and Robert. The white guys called them Willie and Bubba.

William said, "Them white boys think we don't like bein' called Willie and Bubba. They think we hate 'em for it. They's right too, but that's not the only reason we don't like 'em. When we're up there on the dock workin', you best call us Willie and Bubba. Probly git in some bad trouble if you don't."

William had a wife who lived back at the shack with him, and Robert had a girlfriend who lived uptown. Sometimes the girls–Betty and Ella– would come to the river at night and bring their men food. The girls liked that I'd rather hang out with the four of them instead of with my own kind, so they started bringing extra food and would give me some. I'll tell you what - those two girls could cook. I had some of the best food I ever tasted. Sometimes, when I asked what they were giving me, they'd just giggle and say, "No sense knowin' what you're eatin'. Probly ruin your appetite if ya did."

Once the white guys realized I was spending evenings at the river, they started treating me worse. I was always getting bumped or shoved or cussed at. They'd chant, "Yankee Boy, Yankee Boy, Yankee Boy," trying to get me mad. But being friends with William and Robert soon helped me out. They spread the word among the others that I was ok. All those black guys would help me, show me work shortcuts, and give me a hand when a bale was too heavy. Once the white guys found out the blacks would stand up for me, it got a lot easier for me. They pretty much left me alone after that. They still wouldn't call me Rusty though–nothing but "Yankee Boy."

I didn't mind the work much. It was hard, but it kept my mind off my troubles. I didn't like being around all the fighting, yelling, and cussing though, and decided to get out of there as soon as my boots were paid off and I had a little money saved. It couldn't happen soon enough.

It took me almost three months, but I left the night I made the final boot payment.

I had told William and Robert I would be leaving in the morning. They wanted to talk me out of it but knew I wouldn't stay. I think they would have asked to go with me if I had even known where I was going.

"Here's some fried chicken, pork rinds, and biscuits. The girls wanted to give you somethin' for the road." Robert grinned.

I didn't like the South much. My boots and money were stolen here, I had worked on the dock with a bunch of evil men and saw how black people were treated. I didn't want to be around that kind of evil ever again. I needed to put this place behind me.

I started walking East.

Chapter 12

I had never seen mountains before. I heard someone say the mountains in the East were blue, so I wanted to see them. I decided to walk until I was standing in the middle of them. I wanted to stand at the top of one and look in all directions and see nothing but mountains.

I walked for almost a month. I stopped whenever my money got low and I'd work a little–sometimes just a day, sometimes several. I learned my lesson in Memphis though. Now I only stopped in small towns and worked in a store or at an odd job. Sometimes I helped a farmer and got paid with a meal or some food. No more big cities and no more work crews. I promised myself I'd never do that again. Time started to ease the pain of Hidden Spring, but not the memories.

Somewhere east of Beech Grove, Tennessee, I helped a nice farmer plant the last of his corn. He tried to get me to work all summer. "Why don't you stay on, son? I could use the help. Got a lot of haying comin' up and I'm getting too old to do it all by myself. I can pay you a little and you already had a couple of Martha's meals, so you know you're going to eat good. I've got a little place fixed up in the old house. You could have it all to yourself."

"I'm not ready to settle. I've come this far to see the mountains and I intend to see them before I stop. Maybe I'll come back through after that." I knew I wouldn't. He knew too.

I stopped just outside Chattanooga. I had promised myself, no more big towns, but I didn't see a way around it, so I spent the night in a small roadside park and got up before dawn. I was going to walk through the city without stopping if at all possible.

As soon as I passed through, the hills got steeper, and the roads got curvier; I knew I was getting close. I stopped at a general store in a little town in Tennessee named Ocoee. By now the boots I got in Memphis were almost worn through already. I was going to need a new pair before I got to the mountains.

"Where you headed, son?" a lady in a little country store asked, with a husky voice.

She was short and heavy with her gray hair pulled back under a red headscarf. She looked nothing like Miriam, who was a tall, slender woman with a warm smile. But she struck my heart anyway.

"I aim to see the Blue Mountains, ma'am," I told her.

"You got plenty of food?" she asked. "Not many places to stop up there."

"I have a little."

"A little food don't go very far up there. A guy can get awful hungry. Gets cold too. You got a heavy enough coat?"

Her name was Clara. She let me work a few days for supplies. I bought a bigger pack from her too, since I was going to have more to carry. I worked evenings at her sister Wilma's, cafe serving meals and washing dishes. The café was closed on Tuesdays, so I spent one day repairing the front door because it wouldn't shut all the way. One of the hinges was broken and the screws wouldn't hold in the other two. I told them what stuff I needed to fix it, and once they got the material and hardware for it, I went to work. It was an easy fix. The girls paid me with two meals a day and the supplies I asked for. I worked for almost three weeks, but once I had everything I needed, it was time for me to move on.

"You can stay on a bit if you want to," Clara said. "We've got lots of stuff needing done. We wasn't doin' too bad for a while after our husbands died. But then business got bad 'cuz of the depression. My boy Nate and Wilma's boy Jimmy went off and joined the Civilian Conservation Corps. They couldn't find no work around here so's they left. Both promised to send money home, but we ain't seein' many letters. We could use a man around for a while."

I thought about it. I would've stayed like they asked me, but staying here would be too much like our general store in Hidden Spring. "I'm sorry ladies, but I've got this urge and I haven't settled with it yet," I told them.

They fed me a big breakfast, then I cleaned up the cafe and gathered my stuff. Clara and Wilma stood, arms around each other, waving until I was out of sight. I looked back but couldn't wave. I didn't like leaving them alone and needing help, but I couldn't stay.

I hoped that today would be the day that I saw the Blue Mountains. They call them The Blue Ridge here, but the walk along Lake Ocoee was so foggy I could only see a couple of hundred feet. The road was so narrow, I had to worry more about watching for traffic than looking for mountains.

By noon the fog had burned off and I could see for miles. The views I saw made the whole trip worthwhile. I wondered why more people didn't live here. But I was glad they didn't. Seems like people ruin the pretty places.

The road followed a river and each time I rounded a curve, I was greeted with a new scene - each more spectacular than the last. The blue tops of each mountain were surrounded by big puffy white clouds. It was prettier than any picture I'd ever seen in any magazine.

I spent the next few days wandering. I found a trail that led up the side of a mountain to a place called Clingman's Dome and walked to the top. I spent nights up there on top. Waking to the sunrise in the cold and mist was exhilarating. I hiked around during the day, just sightseeing. There were little waterfalls everywhere. I'd seen a lot of hills while walking, but never anything like this. The air was so crisp, and the sky so clear it made me wonder how can life be so hard in such a beautiful world. Still, this wasn't a place where I could stay. There wasn't any work up here, and I'd need to leave before I needed more supplies.

I wanted to find a pretty place–a place where I could work for room and board and be able to explore. Come morning I ate with the sunrise, packed my bag before the sun got warm, and climbed back down the mountain, following the urge that had kept me moving on.

Still, these mountains held me with a force I hadn't felt before. For the first time, I started to feel I could someday find a place to settle.

I spent a few days in a town named Cherokee, on an Indian reservation.

I didn't understand why I didn't see any Indians. A river runs through the middle of Cherokee. There was a park with benches on both sides of the water. I sat for hours and watched the river flow. The water seemed to be fearlessly headed toward an unknown destination. The river doesn't know where it's going, but, without fear, it keeps flowing tirelessly. It reinforced my will and gave me the strength to keep moving on.

At Fines Creek I stopped to rest. I found a store with a sign on the front that read simply, "Good Eats." The store had a couple of Standard Oil gas pumps under a canopy. An old green tractor sat off to the side. A skinny old man wearing a pair of bib overalls over a dirty, torn tee-shirt sat sideways on a bench that looked like a church pew, drawing deep drags off his cigarette. The man pushed his wrinkled fedora back off his forehead, looked up, and said, "You look like you need to sit a spell." His cigarette dangled from the corner of his mouth as he spoke.

"Good morning, sir," I said.

"Folks round here all call me Jim," he answered. "What they call you?"

"Folks call me Rusty, Jim," I answered.

"Where ya headed, Rusty?" he asked.

"Well sir, I guess I don't know now. I came here to see the Smoky Mountains. I guess I don't know where I'm going next," I told him.

"Don't need to go nowheres else, Rusty. It don't git no better'n right here. I bin here all my life and never felt no need to go anywheres else. I bin sittin' on this here bench most ever day for over ten years. Talked to all kinds o' folks from all kind o' places. Don't none of 'em places they talk about sound no better 'n right here," he said. "May as well plant yer feet right here, son."

"No thanks. I think I'll just get something from inside to eat then move along. It sure is pretty here, I'll give you that. But there are lots of mountains to see and I have only seen a few," I said.

"Well then, best git yerself inside and have Sadie fix ya up a mess."

He pulled his hat back down over his eyes before I could even open the front door. Cigarette smoke rolled from under the brim and rose gently to the roof of the canopy.

Inside, there were several aisles with shelves reaching to the ceiling on both sides. Canned goods, clothes, fishing supplies, fresh produce, and a lot more stuff piled randomly throughout. Miriam would have a fit if she saw this mess. I saw the sign over an open doorway and walked through into Sadie's Place, where a big black lady wearing a red polka dot head-scarf and greasy apron was cooking bacon and eggs on an open fire grill. A pile of home fries was stacked off to the side. She looked up from her grill, smiled, and asked, "What's yer name, young'n?"

"Folks call me Rusty, ma'am," I told her.

She was cooking the thickest bacon I ever saw, "Sit yerself down, Rusty. The name's Sadie. I'll fix ya up with some bacon and eggs. Ain't right for a body to be hungry. You need to git some meat on them bones," she said with a warm smile.

Her food was too good to eat just once and I wasn't in any hurry, so I spent the day exploring the area, then spent the night sleeping next to the stream, just so I could eat another helping before I left the next morning.

I stuffed myself. It might be a long time before I had cooking this good–maybe never.

As I got up to leave, she said to me, "I fixed you a little something for the road, son. A man can get hungry for bacon while he walks. Good for the mind too." She grinned a big toothy grin as she handed me a sack.

"Stop by on your way back through," she called. "Bacon's always cookin' here at the Fines Creek Store."

I wanted to say goodbye to Jim, so I hung around for a few minutes, but he didn't show this morning, so I walked on.

Today, the idea of settling for a while took hold. I was tired of traveling. The only time I had someone to talk to was when I stopped somewhere. I was lonesome and homesick, but I didn't have a home.

Day after day, I had walked alone. I missed the farm. I missed Mama and Janie. I missed Moose. I missed Ray and Miriam and Joey and Mary.

I walked through two towns named Trust and Luck. It seemed like an omen to me–Trust and Luck. Was it time for me to trust my luck?

Chapter 13

*T*he sun dropped below the horizon as I entered Hot Springs. Tired and hungry, I found a big old oak tree. I dropped my pack, laid my hat on it, and flopped on the ground next to that oak tree. Eventually, I mustered the energy to pull off my boots and socks. I dug out my water bottle, took a long drink, leaned against the tree, and closed my eyes.

The warm rays of the sun woke me. The smell of coffee brewing and rolls baking brought me to my senses. The sign above the door read *Kitty's Kafe, Best Home Cooking in Hot Springs*. Broke and hungry, I followed the smell coming from across the street.

Inside, customers firmly glued to their chairs were finishing their meals and drinking the last of their coffee before mustering the energy to meet their day. I was overwhelmed by the sweet aroma of freshly baked biscuits when I first opened the front door. I stood for a moment waiting, but no one came to greet me. No one was waiting on customers either. It was obvious that breakfast was over. My weary bones had caused me to sleep too long.

Hunger pains drove me toward the kitchen door. I peered through and was surprised to see only two women working. "Excuse me, I wonder if I might get some breakfast?"

It was immediately clear who was in charge. She was a short, slender lady with dark sparkling eyes and dark brown hair done up in a scarf. She looked up and said curtly, "I'm sorry, breakfast is over. We will reopen at 11:30 if you would care to come back for lunch."

"I'd be glad to work for anything you might have left over. I don't have any food left and I need a job."

"I can round you up some biscuits, still have a little gravy left too. I can warm up a slab of ham to go with it if you want, but you'll have to finish with the last of the customers; clean the tables and help wash up first."

"That would be great, but can I eat first? I'm starved."

"Work first, then you eat. That's the way it works here," she said. "But the first thing you need to do is clean yourself up. I won't have a ragamuffin working around my customers. There's a sink back there. Wash your face and hands, get one of the coats from the closet, and put on an apron."

"Yes ma'am!"

"Call me Kitty. What's your name, Ragamuffin?"

"Folks call me Rusty, ma'am."

"Nice name, matches your beard and red hair, but I'm still gonna call you Ragamuffin anyway," she grinned.

It was nearly two hours before the last of the customers were gone. Once the room was empty, I cleared all the tables and set them up for lunch. I washed the dishes and stacked them neatly on the shelves. It took me quite a while, but it seemed like a real bargain when she set a plate of the best biscuits and gravy ever in front of me.

Kitty's Kafe was the biggest building on Main Street. It originally had been a meeting house of some sort; probably a Grange Hall or Masonic Lodge. The inside was one large open room with a small kitchen carved out of one corner in the back. It had some old pictures on the walls– photos from the earlier days in town–flood pictures, pictures of folks dressed in their Sunday best posing in front of their buggies, and pictures of buildings no longer standing. The tables were a mix–some round, some square, and a couple of long ones. One thing they had in common–none had a matching set of chairs.

Kitty was open six days a week for breakfast and lunch. She started serving at 5 am, closed from 9:30 till 11:30, then reopened for lunch and they shooed the last of the customers out by 3. She and her helper Sarah ran the place by themselves. She started baking biscuits every morning at 3 am and was exhausted by 3 pm. She didn't have a printed menu. Breakfast was biscuits and gravy, scrambled eggs, bacon, and fried potatoes. Lunch was fried chicken, baked beans, mashed potatoes and gravy, coleslaw, and cornbread. Breakfast came with coffee and lunch with sweet tea. Water came with either meal.

She didn't serve meals either early or late. If you came early, you stood outside and waited. If you came late, you were out of luck. Sundays the cafe was closed. No exceptions were made.

"You're welcome to stay on for a while if you'd like. I can't pay you much, but you can eat all your meals here and there's a bed upstairs where you can sleep," she said.

I needed money badly, but I needed food and a place to eat more. "Thanks, you won't be sorry, I promise. I'm good help," I told her.

"Come out back when you're done cleaning up, Ragamuffin. I'll give you a haircut, then you can shave in the basin. Tomorrow, we start at five and I want you to look good for the customers."

The next morning I woke to wonderful smells swelling up from below. I rushed downstairs to a kitchen that was already bustling with activity. Kitty and Sarah (a taller blond girl with a big smile) were so used to the routine that they moved about in silence. Each knew exactly when the other needed a hand and was there precisely at the right time. I wanted to help but it was clear I was just in the way.

"Get those tables set Ragamuffin, we have customers waiting at the door," Kitty commanded without even looking up.

Moments later she appeared from the kitchen, looked around, smiled, and nodded with approval as she walked to the front door to a rush of hungry eaters.

The next three hours were chaos. Locals seated themselves. Visitors hesitated at the door before being shown an empty chair with the simple wave of a hand by someone already seated. Groups were split by the availability of seats and were welcomed into the conversations of each table. Total strangers fell into the routine. Each learned to take their dirty plate and silverware to a bin by the kitchen door, then pay at the window before leaving. No menu meant no check. Everyone's bill was the same.

I set a fresh place complete with coffee and water before the next waiting person could sit. All this with the constant call of "Order up," coming from the kitchen window.

I learned my job on the fly that day. Each time I turned from the window —two steaming plates of biscuits and gravy, a heap of scrambled eggs, a pile of fried potatoes all covered with gravy dripping from the edge of the plate, and a slab of ham on the side—a regular customer would shout and point, "They're next, over here."

I watched in amazement as folks would get the coffee pot and fill every cup at their table, then hand the pot off to another. They poured until the pot ran dry, then started a fresh brew and put it back on the burner. Somehow, Kitty had trained her customers.

By 8 o'clock, the frenzy started to subside. By nine, there were empty seats. At 9:30 Kitty closed the serving window, walked to the front, and hung the *Closed* sign in the window.

She smiled approvingly at me as she headed back to the kitchen. "You did good today, Ragamuffin," she said.

"Is it always like this?"

"Always," she smiled. "You better come to the kitchen and grab a bite; you'll need more energy for lunch."

I spent the next two hours feverishly ridding up, washing dishes, mopping the floor, and setting fresh tables for the noon rush.

At 11:30, she appeared from the kitchen, changed the sign, and opened the door to a second frenzy almost exactly like the first. The only differences were sweet tea had replaced coffee and each plate now was heaped with fried chicken and mashed potatoes instead of ham and eggs. Biscuits smothered with gravy were still served on the side.

At precisely 2:30 she came through the kitchen door, walked to the front, and hung the *Closed* sign. The last of the customers was again shooed from The Kafe. By 5 I had the dishes all washed and put away, the floor swept and the room put in order. I collapsed in a corner chair with a glass of tea.

"Care if we join you?" I looked up to see Kitty and Sarah, each with a glass of tea, each looking much spryer than me, and each bearing a smile of satisfaction and appreciation.

They flooded me with a thousand questions, starting with, "Where y'all from?"

I answered most somewhat reluctantly, with just enough information to satisfy their inquiries. By the time they were done, they knew more about me than anyone but Miriam and Ray. I was surprised that I felt so at ease with two total strangers. I thought I might stay here for a while. Maybe this is the place?

I soon fell into the routine. Breakfast and lunch became organized chaos that I thoroughly enjoyed. The food was good. No - the food was great. The customers all left happy. This place was a diamond in the rough. Strangers –and there were a lot of them–hadn't had a meal like this for days or weeks. Some stayed, as I had, for a second meal; sometimes more. I soon became aware of the reason for the steady flow of new customers. It was *The Trail.*

The Trail– as it was known locally–is more correctly known as The Appalachian Trail. The federal government had built a hiking trail through the Appalachian chain of mountains and it happened to pass just north of town. It was open to hikers even before the CCC completed their construction of campsites and rest stops along the trail. It ran from central Maine to northern Georgia. It is almost twenty-two hundred miles long. Experienced hikers can walk the entire trail in as little as five months. Beginners–newbies as I soon learned to call them–might take seven months to a year to hike the entire trail. Few attempted to hike the whole way and even fewer completed it. Most started somewhere in the middle and quit long before reaching the other end. People started on what they thought would be an adventure and soon learned it was an ordeal.

Hot Springs was about three-fourths of the way from the top, so it was a popular stop. It was a location where those who started at the beginning stopped and questioned their resolve; a halfway stop for the majority who began in the Pennsylvania, New Jersey, or New York areas; and a decision point for those who started in Georgia and were hiking north. So, in many ways, Hot Springs was sort of a make-or-break point for the hikers. By the time they arrived here, many of them were sick of trail food, tired of walking, and lonely. They were questioning their decision and their will to continue.

Word about Kitty's had spread up and down the trail and The Kafe had become a must-stop for rest, rejuvenation, and "good eats." Hikers–mostly young college students–trudged down Main Street drawn by the smell of real home cooking. Groups–sometimes including as many as 20 individuals laboring under the weight of huge packs–collapsed in the shade of the oak trees that lined the streets. Some would lay against their packs; others would lean against a tree or porch railing.

The benches in front of Kitty's and the general store across the street were always full. Occasionally a heated discussion might develop over "seat rights." All took their boots off as soon as they collapsed. They almost looked as though they were part of an endless death march.

I spent some time making the upstairs "my space," then began to fix up The Kafe'. The big room consisted of a bunch of tables and chairs that she had acquired over time. Some were donated, some came from auctions and rummage sales, some looked like they were salvaged from the dump. No two tables were alike, none had matching chairs, and most needed some repair. I found one broken table and three chairs behind the Kafe and took them upstairs for repair. Once they were done, I brought them down and put them in place of those most needing repair. Little by little, I repaired all the furniture on the main floor.

Once I had the inside all fixed, I started on the outside. I replaced a step first; customers were having to step around or over a rotted board. I fixed one of the porch posts. Over the years, so many people had leaned against it that it split. The building was so old the porch posts were all roughhewn pine trees. I spent two Sunday afternoons searching the hillsides outside of town before finding suitable replacements. I spent most of a third Sunday afternoon trimming it to length, jacking up the porch, and removing the old one, but it looked nice when I was finished.

"That's nice," Kitty said, hugging me as she looked at the repair. "I was worried someday this old porch was just going to collapse."

I built a third bench for the porch out of a bunch of old planks that lay in an empty lot down the street. Next, I built three rows of hooks on the outside walls for packs. We had a sign on the door asking customers to leave their packs outside, but it was almost completely ignored, partly because they didn't have a good place to leave them and partly because hikers were worried about their safety. But we were to the point where we could hardly maneuver around tables with plates of food because of all the packs on the floor.

Once I had the outside organized, I found two tables and a few chairs at a used furniture store, fixed them, or at least made them sturdy, so I had an adequate supply of spares. I hadn't realized how much I missed working with wood, fixing stuff, making old things good again. I hadn't done anything since I left Hidden Spring. I felt good about being here.

I liked reading the hikers' faces. I could tell their state of mind by their expressions. The happy faces–the few that were still joking and laughing–were going back to The Trail after their meals. The solemn, quiet faces were deciding whether to go on. I could tell which ones had been hiking for a while and which had just started. Some from each group still had a look of determination. Others had been hiking and were beginning to ask themselves, "Why am I doing this?" But they weren't ready to admit defeat. They were still going on. Then there were the faces wearing a serious, dejected expression. They were suffering. They too, were asking "Why am I doing this?" But their determination was waning. The answer was no longer clear to them. Finally, there were the broken ones. They usually had traces of past tears on the cheeks. Their faces and clothes were unkempt. Their shoes weren't tied, maybe a lace was broken or missing. Some had even lost their hats. Hats and shoes were the most important clothing. I knew immediately when I saw a hiker missing either that they were done. They'd had enough and were quitting.

Often, the broken ones ignored the pack sign and wore or dragged theirs inside with them. They would lay their packs on the floor and collapse into a chair. With their heads propped up on one arm, they would shovel in their food like it was the first time they had eaten in years. For most, they had probably decided to do this hike without any idea about what was involved and were completely unprepared. This was the first real meal they had eaten since they left home. We called these kids "the quitters." It sounded harsh, and we felt sorry for them, but still, they were quitting.

One morning an unusually dejected quitter staggered in for breakfast on a dreary, rainy morning. Days like this– cold, windy, and rainy–made it easier to be a quitter, and there was no doubt that this kid had made up his mind. He wore his baseball cap down over his eyes. Nearly all hikers wore a full brimmed hat for good reason. He wore no raincoat; his flannel shirt was soaked. One leg of his pants was torn. I imagined a painful scrape on his leg, the kind that burns when it gets wet. His boots were untied. Clothes hung from his disheveled pack. He had no water bottle or whistle hanging from his pack. His pack fell from his clutch about three feet from the table. He made no attempt to retrieve it before he collapsed in a heap into the closest empty seat.

I set his coffee next to his head, put my hand on his shoulder to reassure him, and told him I'd have his breakfast in a minute. He chugged his water in one gulp. Then coffee ran down his chin as he held the cup with two shaking hands. A young couple sat on either side of him and tried to cheer him up as they ate. He did not respond. I watched him, long after he finished his meal, sit and stare at his empty plate. "If you are done, I'll take your plate," I said. He looked up but didn't move.

He sat until Kitty walked to the front and turned the sign from *Open* to *Closed* and we began to prepare for the noon meal. I didn't see him leave, but when I was cleaning around that table, I discovered he left his pack. We had a shelf on the wall where we put abandoned items. Most times people returned to claim things like canteens, hats, and gloves. Jackets, shirts, and socks usually stayed throughout the week and were discarded Saturday. Packs were almost always claimed within hours, if not minutes.

I put the pack on the shelf, expecting him to knock on the door wanting to claim it.

He didn't.

Toward the end of lunch, he reappeared; found a seat, and ordered a meal. I pointed to the shelf, "You left your pack," I said.

He merely nodded.

I tried to start a conversation as I brought him another glass of water. "What's your name?" I asked.

"Mike," was all he said.

"Have you been hiking long, Mike?" I asked.

"Yeah, seems like forever. I started in Pennsylvania," he said. "I want to go home. How do I get out of here?"

"You are in Hot Springs, North Carolina. Do you have someone who can give you a ride or come get you?"

"I just want to go home. Don't you have a train or a bus or something?" he asked.

"There's a bus depot back by the bridge you walked over to get to town," I told him.

"Thanks," he said. "Did I leave my stuff here this morning?"

"Yes, your pack is on the shelf against the wall."

Slowly he rose and hobbled toward his pack. I watched as he dragged it back to his table, dug out a pair of sneakers, and started to change shoes. I left him to go back to serving the other customers. In a few minutes, I saw him leave. It wasn't until I came to take his plate that I realized he left his pack and boots again.

I ran to catch him, but he was already out of sight.

I put the boots and pack on the end of the shelf, out of the way. I knew he would never come back.

Chapter 14

I soon understood why Kitty's Kafé was closed on Sunday. We needed a break. Workdays were long at The Kafé. Time flew by and we all enjoyed our days, but by Saturday, we were worn out. Sunday was our day to relax. None of us went to The Kafé for anything. We couldn't. Hikers hung around all day and if they sensed someone was inside, they started beating on the door, wanting to be fed. We relaxed in Kitty's backyard. To get there, I had to leave by the back door of The Kafé and walk behind other buildings.

Kitty's house was two blocks off the main street. She had a picnic table in the middle of a nice yard under a spreading oak. A row of bushes lined the perimeter and there were several small flower gardens scattered in it. Kitty always saved some fried chicken or ham for our afternoons. She always had a cold salad, some boiled eggs, coffee, and tea in her cooler. We made sandwiches out of the store-bought bread I got from the grocery. Sarah brought her boyfriend and usually a cake or pie her mother had baked. We sat at the table under an old oak and watched the clouds roll by. Every other Sunday was haircut day. "You're looking a little shaggy, Ragamuffin," she would say as she appeared from her door, scissors and comb in hand.

My haircut became quite an ordeal; great care went into every detail. Kitty would snip a little, then step back to observe, comb, then snip a little more. Once she finished, she'd say, "Go wash it, and let's see how it looks." When I returned, there was always a final snip or two before she was satisfied, then she'd run her fingers through it to mess it up and comb it again. "Looks nice. That should last for a couple of weeks," she'd smile.

Haircuts became more and more intimate. As she ran her fingers through my hair, she would brush against me with her body. Now, when we ate outside, she sat on the same side of the table, close to me. Very close.

Once the evenings started getting cooler, we would sit on the couch, listening to the radio. She had a cabinet full of books. I tried to read, but she cuddled next to me and lay her head on my shoulder. "Keep me warm, Ragamuffin," she would beg. She started wearing a robe and covering us both with a blanket when we listened. I liked Kitty. I liked her a lot, but I knew I didn't like her in the same way she liked me.

As the summer rolled on, we could tell that Sarah and her boyfriend Jimmy's romance was getting serious. Most Sundays now they wanted to be by themselves. They would hike the trail up to Lover's Leap or spend their afternoon wading in the river. That left Kitty and me alone, without pie or cake, with no one to talk to but each other. She sat uncomfortably close and asked me more about my past than I cared to tell. Some days we would walk to the trailhead and hike a few miles on it or sit on the sand bar and throw rocks in the water. She insisted on holding hands when we walked. "You're my protector, Ragamuffin," she would say.

As the weather got colder, she began to ask me to stay the night. "It's cold in your room at The Kafé; spend the night with me. We could keep each other warm if you stayed."

I began to dread Sundays. Kitty wanted more from our friendship than I had to give. I felt trapped.

One afternoon when we were cleaning up Kitty said, "I got a letter from my sister Jill in Asheville. She wants me to come down for the Easter weekend. We could both go, it would be fun. We could leave Thursday after we close; drive down there and spend the weekend sightseeing. There are lots of things to do and see in Asheville. Jill and her husband have a furniture store there. We'll put a sign in The Kafé window telling everyone we will be closed Monday."

This surprised me, she hadn't said anything about a sister before and she had never mentioned closing The Kafé for a day for anything.

"What about Sarah? Won't you have to tell her?" I blurted out.

"Oh, I've already talked to her about it. She is looking forward to having some time when she and Jimmy can go house hunting and make plans for their future," she grinned.

"Ok," I stammered.

Thursday evening Kitty had her car ready out front. "Come on, Raga-muffin. Let's get going," she called from the street. "What are you doing with all that stuff?" she asked when I came out of the door carrying my backpack and a blanket.

"I didn't know what to bring. You didn't tell me where we are going to stay tonight." I said, fumbling to get the trunk of her car open.

"You won't need all that stuff. Jill has a spare bedroom we can share," she smiled.

The trip to Asheville was beautiful. We drove through Trust, a place I had already seen, but whizzing past in a car didn't give me time to enjoy like before when I was walking. We turned on to a different highway for the ride to Asheville. The mountains were the same here, the road con-tinually curved. It seemed like we were always either going up or down. Kitty was laughing as she pointed things out, talking constantly about Jill and her husband Larry. "You'll like Larry, he's so much like you, shy and sweet. You'll like Jill too; people have always told us we could be twins. I can't wait for you to meet them."

Jill and Larry were standing and waiting on their porch when we arrived. Jill came bouncing down the steps and ran wildly to Kitty. I watched as they hugged for the longest time. Kitty was right–they could be twins. They were so much alike. I couldn't tell who big sister was and who was little.

"Here, let me help you with your bags," Larry offered. "My name is Larry. Jill and I are happy to meet you. Jill has told me a lot about you. We're so glad Kitty finally has a man around."

I immediately knew I would like Larry, but what he said about Kitty having a man made me uncomfortable. I wondered what Kitty had told Jill in those letters.

"We're looking forward to showing you around Asheville. We love it here. It's a great place to live and work and the countryside is spectacu-lar," he continued, then added, "You brought a lot of stuff for just a two-day stay."

The four of us spent the afternoon on their porch. Kitty and Jill were laughing and talking so much it was hard for either Larry or me to say anything.

As the sun began to get low, Jill said, "Let's go downtown. We can show you how pretty it is and drive past our store. We know a nice quiet restaurant. I'll bet you two would like to have a meal prepared for you and served to you by a waiter for a change."

They took us to a nice restaurant. It was in an older neighborhood close to downtown. The building reminded me of Mr. Kerr's General Store in Stockport. It was one big, long room with a high ceiling. The room was about three times longer than it was wide. Lights hung from the ceiling on long poles. There was a row of booths on both sides; the center was filled with tables. The place was busy, but not nearly as busy as Kitty's was every day. The waiter brought us water as soon as we sat and laid menus in front of each of us. Kitty sensed that I was uncomfortable, so she said, "Jill, we don't know what's good here, would you order for us?"

The waiter handed me a wine list. "Would you care for some wine, sir?" I had never seen a wine list before and it must have been obvious.

"We'll all have sweet tea," Larry said.

Once the waiter left, Jill started talking. "Rusty, Kitty has been telling me in her letters what a lifesaver you have been for The Kafé. She goes on and on about how you enjoy the people and how you can repair about anything. She tells me about how she so looks forward to Sundays and your times together. She tells me how much she likes you."

Before I could think of a response, Larry took over the conversation. "Jill and I are overwhelmed at the store now. People are moving to Asheville from all over. There are jobs here, the weather is great, and the scenery is wonderful. Of course, you both know about the weather and scenery. My point is, we want to expand the store. Tomorrow Jill and I would like to take you through it, show you what we do, and see if you might be interested."

"Interested in what?" I asked.

"Just wait until tomorrow. Once you've seen, we can talk more," Larry answered.

Our waiter brought the meals. He set a huge plate of spaghetti in front of me, covered with a white sauce filled with chicken, mushrooms, peppers, and onions. Another waiter brought a whole loaf of bread and a bowl of butter. I looked at the other plates and saw each of us had enough food for two meals. I must have had a surprised expression because Kitty said, "Don't worry, you don't have to eat it all. We can take what we don't eat home and finish it later. They'll bring us little boxes for the leftovers."

I smiled at Kitty. The only thing I could think to say was, "They sure have a lot of waiters here."

She smiled, "Don't get any ideas. The Kafé is doing just fine."

We carried our boxes of leftovers to the kitchen when we got back to their house. As Jill put them in the icebox, she said, "We can have these for lunch tomorrow or Saturday. We'll be too busy to cook." Then she and Kitty shared a grin as she said, "Rusty, you and Kitty can share our spare bedroom if you like?"

"Or, we have a couch that unfolds into a bed if you would rather?" Larry said when he saw that I was caught off guard and uncomfortable with the idea.

"The couch will be fine," I stammered.

We sat and talked until late, Kitty next to me holding my hand while she and Jill talked nonstop. Jill did most of the talking. "You can help us run the store. After a while, you can buy in with us if you like. You are going to love it here in Asheville,; there's so much to do. We bought the building next to ours so we can expand. We are going to open the wall between; Rusty, you can do that. We'll have twice as much room. Asheville is growing so fast. People are coming here to vacation. We have several golf courses. Are you sure Sarah and her sister will buy The Kafé?"

This was the first I heard about Kitty wanting to sell The Kafé. She squeezed my hand, turned to me and said, "You remember, I told you Sarah asked me about buying The Kafe' after she and Jimmy get married. I told you Sarah and her sisters were going to run it."

Kitty moved my hand to my lap as she talked, to comfort me I guess, but she hadn't told me about selling The Kafé and we both knew it.

I awoke to the sound of laughter. My first thought was that it was coming from Kitty and Sarah getting ready to open The Kafé, but when I raised my head and looked around, it was Kitty and Jill in the kitchen fixing breakfast. "Good morning Ragamuffin, did you have a good sleep?" Kitty laughed.

I nodded and began to rub the sleep from my eyes. I was surprised she called me Ragamuffin in front of her sister; I wish she hadn't. I wanted to be called Rusty when we were in public.

"Here, have one of Jill's biscuits. They're so good."

Larry came down the stairs still wearing his pajamas. I watched as he stumbled into the kitchen, put his arm around Jill's waist and they shared a kiss. Maybe married life wouldn't be so bad. Jill and Larry are happy. Sarah and Jimmy seem to be looking forward to it too.

Larry brought me a cup of coffee, then got one for himself and came to the living room, sat in the armchair and grinned at me. "Can't wait to get started this morning. We have so much to show you."

We parked behind the store, but Larry had us walk to the front. "I want your first impression to be a good one," he said. It seemed silly, but they asked us to cover our eyes before they led us inside.

"Ok, you can look," Jill said. "Well, what do you think?"

Kitty was immediately oohing and ahhing, practically skipping from one couch to the next, and sitting in each to check them out. "I like this one; that one is pretty but this one is so comfy. Oh, look at the dining room sets, aren't they nice? I would so like to have one this pretty."

"We aren't here to shop, Sis. This is where we want you to work. We wanted you to see it on Easter weekend, so we could spend time here, just the four of us. Imagine what it looks like when it is filled with customers, and it is filled with customers almost every day," Jill said.

"Come with me you two. Let us show you what we have in mind next door," Larry said, as he ushered us out to their adjacent building.

"We bought this with the idea of doubling our floor space," Jill said as we entered. We walked through the door to find a large, empty room nearly the size of their store, but without fixtures and obviously, without inventory.

"Our idea is to close off the entrance to this building, knock out a large part of the adjoining wall, build an archway for access," Jill said. "If you two are interested in joining us, we thought we might use the back half of this side as a shop. Rusty, you could have a furniture repair shop here. Kitty goes on and on about how handy you are and how good your repairs look. Eventually, you could build custom furniture for the store. We constantly have customers ask for modifications to items we have and want something built to match a piece they are interested in or already own. I can't tell you how many times someone has wanted a table or picture frame to match that just isn't available.

"We can put a sign on the front that says *Rusty's Fine Furniture, Custom Made and Repaired*, if you like," Jill went on.

"We know this is a big step. We don't expect answers now, we just want you to consider our ideas. Eventually, if you like what we are doing, we would be glad to have you as partners; but I know I am thinking too far ahead," Larry said.

"Rusty, you could pick up and deliver your repair jobs. You could also make on-site estimates. We are also frequently asked to come to the home to make suggestions. This is something Jill often does. It may be something you and Jill could do together."

This all was overwhelming. Kitty hadn't told me anything about this weekend other than she wanted to see her sister. She and Jill had apparently been talking about this for a long time, but she hadn't said a word about it to me. Also, she had been talking to Sarah and Jimmy about taking over The Kafé and I didn't know anything about that either. She made plans, or at least assumptions, about our future together. My mind was spinning.

Once I realized they were all expecting me to respond, all I could manage was, "I don't drive."

"Not a problem," Larry laughed. "I can teach you this weekend. You and I can go for a drive while Kitty and Jill catch up on old times."

We spent the rest of the afternoon looking at their stock and talking about how much inventory they would need after the expansion. Larry told me about his ideas for the store, the repair shop, places Kitty and I might live, and how easy it was to learn to drive. "We need to think about dinner," he finally said. "Jill, let's take them to Arnie's for dinner. Kitty, you and Rusty will love this place, they are famous for their barbeque. Do you like barbeque, Rusty?"

"I had some in Memphis," I answered. "I worked with some black guys there. Their wives sent barbeque for their lunch. It was kind of spicy," I said.

"This place serves it as spicy or mild; either way you want," Larry said.

"Let's finish up here, Jill. We've run a lot past these two today. They've got a lot to think about, and everybody knows you can't think on an empty stomach," Larry said.

I sat next to Larry, across from Kitty and Jill. Arnie's was a great place. I wondered if William and Bob's wives always cooked their barbeque so spicy, or if they were serving it hot to me for fun? I wondered why Kitty hadn't been telling me all that was going on about The Kafé and moving and working in the store. Mostly, I wondered why she was making these plans for us without asking. I knew she felt more toward me than I did toward her. I knew she knew it. I knew that if we were to marry, I was supposed to be the one that asked. This was all happening too fast.

My head was spinning, I needed to be alone with my thoughts.

"You are being very quiet," Kitty said. "We have driven almost halfway to Hot Springs and you haven't said a word."

"I know."

"Well?"

"Well, this is all happening too fast. I didn't even know you were thinking of selling The Kafé to Sarah, and I sure didn't know anything about Asheville."

"I know, but you knew people were pressuring me to serve three meals a day, seven days a week. And since the general store started selling beer, a lot of our customers wanted a beer with their dinner instead of tea. And you know what I think about alcohol. I told you about my dad and his drinking and how much mom hated how he got when he was drunk," she said.

"Yeah, I know, I guess."

"Scoot over here and sit next to me, Ragamuffin. Everything is going to be fine. Everything is going to be better than that, it will be wonderful, you'll see," she said, reaching her arm around my shoulders.

"Want to drive?" she teased.

Chapter 15

*K*itty and Sarah now talked openly about The Kafe changing owner-ship. Jimmy started helping clean in the evenings after his work at the grocery store was done. Two of Sarah's sisters, Ginny and Margie, also started helping. Some days they worked in the kitchen to learn the pro-cess; some days they worked with the customers. Their third sister Alice began as soon as she graduated high school. A June wedding was planned.

"Sarah and I talked about a double wedding, but I said I didn't want to take away from hers. Besides, I think we should get married in Asheville. Jill and Larry could stand up for us," Kitty cooed.

Now, with a greatly reduced workload, I spent my days doing odd jobs. I finished repairing the front porch on the Kafé, built another rack for hik-er's packs, cleaned the walkway, spread some new gravel, repainted signs, cleaned the storage room, stacked firewood, cleaned the back yard, and wondered about my future. Kitty was planning to get married. I hadn't said I wanted to marry her and certainly hadn't proposed, but it didn't seem to matter.

"You should look for a car," Kitty said. "When we move to Asheville, we will need two. Why don't you go drive to Marshall and shop? There's a couple of places there. You need a driver's license now that North Car-olina passed a law. They have a test at the courthouse. You could spend a couple of days," she said.

"I'll go one morning next week, after the first busy spell in The Kafé," I answered.

I hadn't been on the road to Marshall before, but I was now familiar with the type of highways here and had driven Kitty's car enough to be comfortable driving this road. And I wasn't in a hurry. This was the first time I was alone since the trip to Asheville; I had time to think. Time alone was just what I needed, but it didn't last long enough.

By the time I arrived at the courthouse, parked the car, and walked to the licensing department, I had made my decision.

"Next," the clerk called from behind her desk.

I rose from the waiting room chair and moved toward her.

"How can I help you, young man?" she asked, without taking much notice of me.

"I need a driver's license, ma'am."

"You've come to the right place. What's your name and where are you from?"

"I live up in Hot Springs. My name is Russell Jordan. Folks call me Rusty, ma'am."

"Well, first you need to take a written test, Rusty. Iif you pass it, you will have to take a driving test with an officer. If you don't have an auto for the test, we will furnish one."

"Thank you, ma'am. I do have a car for the test."

"Good. Did someone drive you here today?"

"No ma'am, I drove myself."

"Son, am I to understand that you drove here from Hot Springs, on curvy old Highway 25, by yourself?"

"Yes ma'am."

"Here is the written test. If you pass it, we won't have to bother with the driving test," she said. She turned toward the room and called, "Who's next?"

I found a nice Chevy. A green 1933, two-door sedan. It was the same year as James' new Buick, but that was over seven years ago. The man at the car lot told me they would clean it up and hold it until the weekend. "It's got four good tires on it. Don't find that much, what with the govermint rationing rubber 'cause of the war," he said.

I agreed to buy it and told him I'd come back for it next Sunday.

"We are not normally open on Sundays, but since that's the only day you can come back, and since you paid cash for it today, I can meet you here. Will two o'clock work for you? I'll have it all cleaned up and have a full tank of gas," he said.

On the way back I saw an island in the middle of the river and stopped. There wasn't anybody around. I removed my shoes and waded through the cold water and found a rock where I could sit and let the water rush through my feet. It was a good place to think.

"How'd your day go, Ragamuffin?" Kitty asked.

"Good, I got my driver's license, found a car, and bought it. I'll need you to drive me back to Marshall Sunday to pick it up," I said.

"That sounds great. We can leave right after your haircut. You are starting to look shaggy like you did when you first came here five years ago. And that beard...what's with that? I don't like it; we'll shave it on Sunday too."

"No, I think I'll keep it for a while. We can put off the haircut too. It feels good to let it grow a little. I like it."

"Well, I don't," she said sternly, frowned, and left the room.

Chapter 16

*W*e didn't talk much on the trip to Marshall to pick up my car. We didn't talk about The Kafé or Sarah and her wedding. We didn't talk about Asheville and we didn't talk about moving.

After a long silence, she asked me about the car.

"It's green," I told her.

We went for Sunday rides in my new car after that. We drove up along the river and into Tennessee. One Sunday we drove up to where Douglas Lake was going to be built. It was sad to see all those farmhouses in the bottom, knowing those folks were going to lose their farms and all that good topsoil. We drove down through Trust and Luck to Fines Creek. I was avoiding Sunday haircuts and Sunday evening meals. That last evening, after The Kafé closed for the day, I carried my pack and extra clothes to the car and hid them under a blanket in the trunk. Then I went back to my room to write letters.

First, I wrote to Sarah:

I am sorry that I will miss your wedding. I would like to see you and Jimmy say your vows, but I think it will be best for Kitty if I'm not there. You will understand once you talk to her. I wish you and Jimmy all the best and hope you and your sisters do well with The Kafé. I have repaired everything I could think of, so hopefully, your first few months will be profitable and uneventful,

Rusty

Then, I wrote to Larry:

I regret to tell you that I won't be moving to Asheville with Kitty. I am not ready for this kind of change. I am writing to tell you this now before you start setting up your new addition, so you will have the chance to change plans to suit your needs. I will never forget your kindness.

Rusty

///

Finally, I wrote to Kitty:

As you read this letter, you will already know that I am gone. I like you a lot, more than I can express; but I don't love you in the way you love me. It would not be fair to either of us to continue our relationship. I can't be married to you and we can't be just friends. I hope you find someone to make you happy. I am sorry I am not that person. I wish you all the best.

Love, Rusty.

I wished I hadn't told her that first day when I came to town,"You won't be sorry," because I knew, when she read my note, she would be.

I waited until I saw Kitty's lights go out, then I laid the letters for Kitty and Sarah on the counter in the kitchen, locked the front door, and pointed the green Chevy south.

I wanted to start by driving through Trust and Luck. They had been a good omen for me before and hoped they would be good again. I stopped at the Fines Creek store. It was still early. It wasn't open yet, but I wanted another one of Sadie's bacon sandwiches. I parked across the road, facing the store, leaned back in the seat, and tried to sleep.

The warmth of the morning sun woke me, just like all those mornings before when I was traveling. Jim drove up to the side of the store, parked his truck, unlocked the front door, and sat on his bench in front. A young girl arrived shortly. I watched as she turned on the inside lights and fiddled with the cash register. I waited and waited, but the black lady never arrived. Finally, thinking she must come through the back door, I walked across the street to go in. The man on the bench greeted me.

"Howdy, son. Fixin' to be a warm one. Set yerself down fer a spell. Jaw with me awhile."

"I'm traveling on," I told him. "I came through here a few years ago and stopped for another bacon sandwich. This is a little out of my way, but I couldn't pass up the chance to have another," I said.

"Sorry to disappoint you son, but yer too late. Sadie, she up an' died last week. Took sick and was gone afore we could even git her to a doctor. Don't know what she died of. Too bad she's gone, she'd a 'membered ya sure. She 'membered ever body. We all miss her. That ol' grill's cold now.

Been cold ever since that morning. Don't know if anybody's ever gonna cook on it agin. Don't seem right neither; someone else cookin' on Sadie's grill."

He finally paused in his monologue. "Got some jerky inside, if ya'd like. Some of them newfangled tater chips too, if'n that'll help."

"No, thanks," I said, dejectedly. "I'm not hungry yet, I just wanted a bacon sandwich and a visit with her."

"Well, I kin do the visitin', but I ain't no cook. Want to sit a spell?" he offered.

"No, thanks," I said again. "I would buy some gas before I leave, though."

"Sorry 'bout that too. Gas man was s'posed to be in here yesterday. Never showed up, though."

"I've got enough to get by. I'll be moving on. Thanks," I said, and walked back to the Chevy.

I sat in my car for a while just thinking, remembering, wondering.

I remembered reading about the Atlantic Ocean in one of Miriam's books. The most water I had ever seen was the Mississippi River at Memphis. I decided driving to see the ocean was as good a way to start as any.

I stopped in Asheville, found Larry and Jill's store, and slid the letter I had written to them through the mail slot, then turned the Chevy east.

Chapter 17

*T*he Smoky Mountains ended close to a little town called Flat Rock. This reminded me of how the Ozark Mountains ended at Marked Tree in Arkansas. I was now driving through valleys with little farms scattered randomly along the road. The blue haze on the hilltops was gone, but this was still pretty country. The little farms made me think about our place on the Cedar back in Iowa. I began to think about Mama and Janie and Moose again. I wondered about Kitty; she had read my note by now. I knew she would be upset, but I also knew that I couldn't go back, and I didn't want to.

Traveling by car was completely different than walking. No one came out to the fence to visit as I passed. No one asked if I needed a drink or a meal. No one even noticed me. I felt more alone than at any time since Mama died and Janie got stolen. I began to realize something else; no one was going to offer me a place to sleep or an evening meal. With a car, I could go further than on foot, but since I didn't have a place to go, having a car wasn't much of an asset. I was going to have to buy gas and find a place to park every night and since I was traveling by car, jobs were going to be harder to find.

The sun began to get low in the sky behind me. For the first time in years, I wouldn't see it fall into the blue haze, then vanish behind the Appalachians. The valleys with little farms had given in to flat lands with endless fields. Farmhouses were now pushed against the road; the land in the valleys was too precious to waste on sprawling outbuildings. The little towns now had many businesses: groceries, hardware stores, implement dealers, and more. People seemed to be in a hurry here. I watched parents pack several kids in the cab of their pickups after filling the back with sacks of feed or groceries. In South Carolina, I drove through towns with names like St. Matthews, Providence, and Holy Hill.

I found what was called a motor court in the little town of Wide Awake and decided to try it. It was close to Charleston and the ocean. I rented a small cabin; for two dollars I got a heated room with a kitchenette and free breakfast. There were a few pots and pans, four plates, and some silverware in the drawers, but I didn't have anything to cook. My money won't last very long if every day costs this much.

I walked to a little café next to the motor court. Breakfast was good–not nearly as good as Kitty's–but I ate enough to last me until the evening. I threw my stuff in the trunk and drove toward the ocean, wondering what it would be like. By the time I got there, the sun was already heating the day. I thought I would see long empty beaches of white sand. Instead, there were people everywhere. More than Memphis. A lot more. I didn't find any white sand either. Brush and shrubs grew right to the edge of the water. Then a green moss-like bog extended into the water as far as I could see. I drove north along the shore, but couldn't find a place to wade.

This is the ocean. Why would anyone want to live here? I found a sign that read *Beach Access* and drove toward the water, but there were houses everywhere and no place to park. I drove for almost two hours with houses on one side of the highway and the marsh on the other. At a little town called Myrtle Beach, I found a campground that had access to the water. I parked my car and walked to the office. A little shriveled-up lady with a cigarette hanging from the corner of her mouth greeted me.

"Stayin' for the night or the week?"

"I just want to see the ocean."

"Well, if you're not camping, you can find a parking lot up the street a couple of blocks. If you want to stay here, it'll be two dollars a night or five dollars a week. We don't have no café, but each cabin's got a hot plate and an icebox. There's a public beach with a bathhouse where you can change into your swimsuit. There's restrooms in it and a snack bar facing the water. It'll cost you a dime to park and use the facilities," she said, flicking the cigarette ashes on the floor.

"I don't have a swimsuit. I just want to see the water," I insisted, getting a little frustrated.

"They won't let you go in the water without no swimsuit. They won't let you go in nekkid neither," she smiled.

"I don't know how long I'll stay," I told her.

"Well, they ain't no refunds. You decide, boy."

"Ok, I suppose I can do a week, it's too much to pay by the day."

She took my money without a thank-you. "The name's Harriet if you need anything. Don't come knockin' after nine and don't make no noise neither," she grumbled, then shuffled back to her chair. Smoke rolled around both sides of her head as she walked. She flopped into her chair and disappeared behind her magazine.

I paid the attendant ten cents, found a spot to park the Chevy, and walked around the bathhouse toward the water.

I rolled up my pants legs and took off my shoes and waded to the edge. It was colder than I expected. I stood for a moment, letting my feet adjust to the temperature. As I moved deeper, the waves began to hit my legs. It was an uneasy feeling. I had to brace against the current to keep from falling. Both the cold and the waves made me feel awkward. I had never been in water that moved around like this. The water was almost to my knees and my pants were getting wet from the sloshing. I stood for a moment then saw a bigger wave coming. Before I could turn and start toward shallower water, it hit me full-on, splashing water over my pants and up onto my shirt.

Cold and soaked, I turned to hurry back to shore. A bigger wave hit my back, knocked me over, and threw me down face into the water. I tried to battle the current, but my feet couldn't reach the bottom. The water held me under and tossed me around until I thought I was going to drown. Then as quickly as it hit me, the water was gone. I lay panting and soaked, with water in my eyes and mouth. For a few moments, I just laid there, happy to be alive, not caring about how cold I was.

"First time in the ocean, Fuzzy?" someone giggled.

I rose to my knees and wiped the burning water from my eyes. Three girls stood over me.

"Nice bathing suit," laughed one of the three.

"Yeah, you're supposed to wear a suit, dummy," the first one said, still giggling.

"Aw, leave Fuzzy alone. He's kind of cute," the third one said.

I struggled to my feet, still rubbing my burning eyes.

"My name is Russell; you can call me Rusty."

"You look more like a Fuzzy than a Rusty with that scraggly beard. Maybe we'll see you again, Fuzzy," said the first girl as they turned to leave.

They were laughing and giggling as they skipped down the beach, leaving me standing out of breath and dripping on the sand.

At first, I started to follow them, but when they turned toward a row of beach chairs, I went straight along the shore because I couldn't think of anything more to say and I didn't feel the need to talk to them anyway. As I walked, carrying my shoes, the sand became first warm, then hot. As the sun got higher in the sky, the sand became unbearably hot. I found relief by walking at the edge of the water. But as my clothes began to dry, they stuck to my skin and the salt started to burn. I turned around to walk back toward my car. I needed to find a place to buy a proper bathing suit, then I would give the ocean one more try.

The footprints I had just made were already washing away. I looked at the tracks others were making walking toward or away from me. All tracks were disappearing, all were temporary; they only existed in the minds of those who made them, and only if the track makers thought about them. It made me pause to think.

What trace of me have I left behind? There is only the little footbridge I built over the mud hole on our farm, and if anyone walked across it, they wouldn't know who built it. The garden in Hidden Spring is probably all grown up in weeds by now. Ray's chair may still sit on the porch, and my sign might still hang, but they wouldn't mean anything to anyone who saw them. All I left in Memphis were memories in the minds of a few of the guys. In Hot Springs, there are some repaired tables and chairs, but only Kitty and Sarah know I fixed them.

"Hi Fuzzy," one of the girls called from the beach chairs.

"He's so cute. Don't you think he's cute?" another said.

They were sitting in fancy beach chairs under umbrellas, out of the sun. I looked at them and smiled but didn't return their waves. I just kept on making new footsteps that wouldn't last.

"My, don't you look a sight. Looks like that ole sun and sand kinda got the best of ya'll. Figure on goin' back in? Or ya'll had enough? 'Member, I tole ya, no refunds," Harriet quipped after looking up from her magazine. "There's a little shop up the street called Sherry's. They have bathing suits– men's and women's. They close at five, so ya better git a move on if'n ya'll figure on buyin' one today."

I didn't want another experience like today's, so I walked uptown thinking I should do as she said.

Sherry's place wasn't hard to find. I saw the display of beach umbrellas along the front of the building. I could tell from a distance it was a beach stuff store. People walking on the sidewalk had to maneuver through the maze of tables heaped with towels and toys and coolers and drinking cups. Some were visibly annoyed, but I guess the display worked, because I found the door and walked in. The inside was a maze too. There were rows and rows of brightly colored clothes. Shelves along the walls were full of shoes, hats, and sunglasses. The walls were covered with pictures of pretty girls in skimpy bathing suits. I stood in awe. From the outside, I couldn't fathom all this stuff could be packed into such a small store.

"May I help you find something?" a young woman asked. I turned to see a tall, dark-haired girl wearing a red bathing suit with a see-through jacket over her top. Her hair was pulled back in a ponytail with sunglasses resting on her head. Her dark eyes sparkled under the bright lights in the ceiling. I stood admiring how pretty she was–gawking, I guess.

"Is there something I can help you find?" she repeated.

"A bathing suit," I stammered.

"Is it for you?" she asked.

"Yes, I guess I need a suit to go into the water. This is the first time I have ever been to an ocean."

"I guessed as much," she smiled. "Follow me to the men's section, we can fix you up. Do you know what size you wear?"

"No ma'am, I've never been measured before."

She reached around my waist with a tape measure. Her hair brushed against my face. It smelled so good. "Not a problem, I'll just get some measurements, she smiled. "My name is Janice, what's yours?"

"My name is Russell, but most folks call me Rusty," I answered sheepishly.

"The name fits you perfectly, with that rusty hair and beard," Janice smiled. "Here, what do you think of these?" she asked, holding up a couple of suits.

"They're kind of small, don't you think?" I felt my face get hot, and guessed it must be redder than my hair.

"No, you'll look great in one. All the guys are wearing them. I think this one works best," she went on. "The orange goes great with your hair."

"Ok, if you think that one is best, I'll take it," I said.

"You need a shirt and hat to go with it. You'll probably want some sunglasses too. It gets pretty hot out there," Janice said. "Come over here, I know just the shirt. It'll go great with your new suit."

I tried to protest. "I'm just here for a couple of days; I just need a suit," I said.

In a few minutes, I found myself standing in front of a big mirror looking at a guy–me–wearing a bathing suit, a colorful shirt, a new hat, and a pair of sunglasses sticking out the shirt pocket.

"You're looking pretty slick, Rusty. I get off work in a couple of hours; come down to the beach and I'll introduce you to the gang. We have a party every evening. There'll be all kinds of good things to eat and drink. . Later we'll start a fire, sit around and talk…tell stories, you know. You shouldn't miss it, we have lots of fun; you'll have a great time," Janice said."Here, let me put your clothes in a bag," she added as she started picking up my stuff.

"I'll just change back to my old stuff."

"No, you've got to wear your new outfit. You look real sharp; everyone will notice your new look."

She was so nice and such a help; I couldn't argue. I waited as she filled the bag with my old clothes, then followed her to the cash register to pay.

As I walked to the door, she called, "Remember–tonight, five-thirty, on the beach. We have lots of fun. See you there!"

"Well, ain't you just the lady killer in them new duds," Harriet yelled as I passed on my way to my cabin. "Looky out there, gals. There's a hot one out on the town tonight."

Even after I shut the cabin door, I could hear Harriet out there hollering, making fun of me. I took my new beach clothes off, dug my old pants and shirt out of the bag, and put them on. I stuffed the beach clothes in the bag and tossed it in the corner.

What was I thinking? What am I doing here, anyway? I turned off the bathroom light and sat in the quiet and stared at my small view of the ocean. For the first time in what seemed like forever, I thought about Mama's Bible. I wished I still had it. I wondered if I should have gone back to look for it after the man in the truck had left. He might have tossed it out of his truck. But I hadn't seen any of my other things as I walked toward Hidden Spring that next day. I guess there wasn't any reason to think it could still be out there somewhere. But deep down I knew it had to be somewhere; just like Janie was somewhere out there.

Chapter 18

*T*he morning sun began to warm my body. I rubbed my eyes and realized I had fallen asleep in the chair. The bag of clothes still lay in the corner where I'd thrown it the night before.

I found the coffee pot in the cupboard– still filthy and full of grounds left by the last tenant. I heated some water on the hot plate, washed the coffee pot with it, and started a brew. Once the coffee was ready, I sat to eat the last two of my boiled eggs, some stale bread and an apple, and watched the sun rise and shimmer over the water through my window. I wished I hadn't slept so long. I wanted to see the sunrise from behind the water's edge and had missed it this morning. Tomorrow I'll see it, I promised myself. I removed the clothes from the bag, hung them on a hook, and put my regular things on.

The sand was cold on my bare feet. Nothing like yesterday afternoon when it was so hot I couldn't bear it. The beach was almost deserted. Umbrellas were all folded, but the chairs were strewn everywhere, some turned over, some in the water. For some reason, the beach seemed narrower this morning. But the water was calm, so I rolled up my pants and waded along the edge. I saw little fish; some darted away, some swam between my feet as I walked. I stooped and tried to catch one, but they were too fast. Small birds scooted along the edge; running out as the waves retreated, then scurrying back as the next wave came in. All the time chirping. It was peaceful here. Just me and the water. I had the same feelings as on those cold mountain mornings back in the Blue Ridge. I found a big rock and sat on it with my feet in the cold water and the warm sun on my face. A couple walked past, wished me a "good morning," and detoured around me. I watched them walk slowly, hand in hand, until they appeared to be just one object. Another couple came to the water's edge and stood ankle-deep, staring at the reflection of the warming sun. Swimmers began to arrive–kids mostly. Little by little, people began to occupy the chairs, moving them under umbrellas. They spread their blankets and coolers to settle in for a day on the beach.

It was becoming crowded, so I left my rock and the beach and returned to the cabin. Harriet was sitting in front of her office, cigarette hanging from her mouth, reading the morning paper. She looked at me over her newspaper, just enough to acknowledge my presence, before dropping her eyes back to the print. I warmed the last of my coffee, moved to the chair in front of the cabin, and nursed it until it was gone.

Later I walked Uptown, looking in the shops, watching families on the street, and found a small grocery store with fresh local fruit. I bought some bread, butter, a quart of milk, a chunk of jerky, some apples and oranges, and took it back to the cabin. I spent the heat of the afternoon leaning against a tree trunk, watching the beach and the people passing by through a little opening in the bushes. As the sun began to wane, I put on my new beach clothes and ventured out for a walk.

The white sand extended for as far as I could see. It was covered with swimmers and waders. Little kids were playing in the surf with their parents watching - sort of. I wandered on, stopping occasionally to watch a child building a sandcastle or young boys roughhousing in the water. I noticed shells thrown about in the water and discovered I could trap them with my foot each time, just as the surf began to recede. I walked and waded and watched while collecting shells until I realized I had gone a long way. I was beginning to get hungry and thought I should return to the cabin for supper. The sun was getting lower in the sky as I turned back. Nothing was familiar. I realized I was lost. But I wasn't really, all I had to do was follow the beach until I saw my cabin. My hunger pangs became uncomfortable. I hadn't eaten since breakfast.

As I approached the cabin, I could see the party Janice told me about yesterday had started. Kids were splashing each other in the surf, playing catch with a football, and sitting with plates of food.

"Hey, Rusty, come join the fun," Janice called from the group. I tried to ignore her, but she persisted. "Come on, we've got lots of extra food," she repeated. She came running toward me, followed by several of her friends. Before I could retreat to the cabin, they were dragging me toward the party.

"Ooh, there's that cutie again," the girl from yesterday grinned. She took me by the hand and pulled me to the center of the crowd. "This is the cutie I was telling you about, girls," she said. "Don't you just love his orange and green shirt? It practically glows in the dark. And that plaid hat is so cool with the feather sticking out of it."

"I'm the one who got him to buy it. The feather was my idea. Isn't he just the handsomest thing you ever saw in his new beach duds?" Janice said. "Come on' Rusty, let's get you something to eat. We've got fried chicken and corn on the cob. Mary made her famous potato salad. Come on, I'll help you fill a plate. You need something to drink too. We've got cold beer, Coke, and rum. I could make you a rum and Coke if you like?"

"I don't drink," I stammered. "I'll just get a glass of water?"

"Water? We've got a whole ocean full of water. What you need is a little lightening up. A rum and Coke will do you good," she said.

I frowned and shook my head no.

When she realized I wasn't going to drink alcohol, or be the life of the party, she frowned. "Well, be that way if you want. The rest of us are here for a good time. Sit over there out of our way if you are going to be a stick in the mud."

I watched them frolic while I ate my meal. The girl who told me I was cute finally came over. "Come on cutie. We have a ball. Play catch with me," she begged. "Then you and me can share my blanket."

I just stared at her mutely, not even wanting to think what sharing a blanket with her might lead to.

"You just sit here; I'll be right back. I'll get you loosened up. My name is Penny, by the way."

I watched as she skipped her way over to a group of kids standing off by themselves. She talked to them a bit, then they all started laughing and looking at me. Penny came back carrying a half-full glass of a clear liquid. I assumed it was water.

"Here, drink this down, then you'll feel better," she urged.

"I don't want it if it's rum," I answered.

"Trust me, it's not rum. It's really sweet, like sweet tea. I know you're going to like it. Here, chug it all at once," Penny said.

"I don't think I should," I said, holding my hand up to push the glass away.

"Aw, come on. It'll do you good. We're all friends here, what could it hurt?" she laughed.

Several of the bunch she had just talked to, were now standing behind her. Each one of them had a glass in their hand. They were all laughing.

"Chug it. Put it up to your mouth and just pour it in. It tastes real sweet. Come on, we'll all do it together," one of the guys said. Then he turned to the others, "Ok, on three, everybody. Come on Rusty, everybody, all together now, one, two, three, chug!"

They all began to chant, "Chug! Chug! Chug! Down the whole thing, Rusty. You can do it. Chug it, man, chug it!"

It tasted sweet as it passed over my tongue and started down my throat. Then it started to burn. Explode, really. I was instantly woozy and disoriented. The world around me started to spin. I couldn't stand. The sand began to rush toward me. My face was the first part of me to hit it. I lay there momentarily, trying to make my arms and legs work, trying to stand up. Then, I felt the most awful retching in my gut. Everything in my stomach started coming back up. The fried chicken, the sweet corn and potato salad—all of it. I vomited again and again until there was nothing left. But even then, I kept throwing up. I couldn't focus on the ground below me. I tried to get to my hands and knees but couldn't. I collapsed in the mess. It seemed that everyone at the party was now surrounding me. I heard Janice laugh, "Looky, everyone, the hick is sick!"

They were all laughing, I could see their feet as they danced around me. A chant started and quickly spread. "The hick is sick. The hick is sick. The hick is sick!"

My world spun wildly, then turned black.

I was starting to feel warm. My eyes hurt when I tried to open them. Then a horrible smell stung my nose and jerked me awake. I tried to move, but my body still wouldn't work right.

I finally lifted my head, managed to get my hands under my shoulders, and push. I was still on the beach. The horrible stench was from last night's vomit. I was laying in it. Slowly, I managed to sit up. The remains of the party were all around: empty beer cans, empty cups, empty plates, and empty lawn chairs. Everyone was gone. Everyone but me.

Most of the stench was on my shirt and it was clinging to my body. I managed to pull it off over my head, but the effort and the smell brought me back to my hands and knees. Suddenly, I started vomiting again, but nothing came out.

The morning beach crowd had begun to gather. Kids came toward me to look before their parents steered them away. Couples stopped momentarily, stared, held their noses and shook their heads. The morning clean-up crews began to work, organizing chairs and umbrellas, picking up cans and bottles, and raking up the trash. They weren't happy as they got closer to me, "You better git yer ass outa here, boy. If you ain't gone in a minute, I'm callin the cops. You and your friends oughta have to clean this mess up. What's the matter with you anyway, don't you got no respect?" one of them yelled, as he came toward me. "And don't be goin' in the water with that puke all over ya neither."

I scrambled to my feet, stumbled and fell a couple of times as I ran for the cabin.

"Git yer ass back here. You ain't leavin' your nasty old shirt for us throw out," a crew member yelled.

As I came stumbling toward the cabin, Harriet looked up.

"Y'all ain't bringin' that stinkin' shirt back in my cabin. Throw that thing away, git yer ass around back behind the office an clean yerself off with that hose. I seen ya layin' out there this mornin'. I know'd what wuz gonna happen soon as I seen you walkin' back from town yesterday wearin' that Gawd awful shirt and that stupid hat. Right then I know'd you'd been in the beach shop 'n either Patsy or Janice sold you that dumb lookin' stuff. What's the matter with you, boy? You stupid or what? You weren't smart enough to see you was the onlyest one chuggin' the moonshine?

"I've seen them kids do this to a buncha you dummies," she kept up her tirade. "They's gonna do it to a bunch more after you. Ain'tcha never heard of no moonshine afore? It's dang near pure alcohol. They got ya to chug it, I'm bettin'. Nobody chugs it dummy. Ya jest sposed ta sip it. Gawd, yer dumb!"

She flicked the ash off her cigarette and went back to reading her magazine. "You'll be checkin' out first light, I reckon."

"No, ma'am," I answered. "I came here to see the sunrise and I've paid for the week. I'm staying."

"Gawd, yer dumb!" she said again.

I had a tough night. My stomach hurt like it never had before. Every time I laid my head on the pillow, the room started swimming around me.

Morning through my little window told me I missed the third sunrise. After a cup of coffee, a glass of milk, and several slices of bread and butter, I found the shirt, sealed it in a bag, and walked toward town. Through the window of the beach store, I could see Janice leaning with her back toward me helping a customer find the right pair of beach shoes. Quietly, I walked in.

I tapped her on the shoulder. She turned, our eyes met and a startled look came over her face. I handed her the bag. "I'm returning the shirt," I said.

Instinctively, she took the bag from me and opened it. The stench hit her full-on. She began coughing and gagging, dropped the bag and began to swear violently at me.

I walked out of the store without turning back.

Later that afternoon, I sat at the edge of the water in my bathing suit without the shirt or hat. The partiers from last night gradually returned. They all avoided me. No one spoke, no one even acknowledged my presence. Peacefully, I sat enjoying the gentle slap of the wave against my legs.

The next morning I rose long before sunrise. I fixed my breakfast and sat quietly eating until the sky began to grow lighter. I walked to the edge of the water to admire the view. Birds began to arrive–first swallows flitted through the air catching insects. Gulls were next–swooping, squawking, filling the air with commotion. Then the shorebirds–those long-legged sand runners that constantly follow the water as it rolls up the sand, breaks, and retreats.

The sun's first glimpse over the horizon gave birth to a new day. That first sliver of orange shot a shaft of fire across the water which followed me as I meandered along the water's edge.

The blue-black clouds gradually came to life, ignited from below by the brightening sky. Gradually, they began changing from a lifeless mono-tint to vibrant oranges, reds, and yellows until the sky began to change to a glowing blue.

The bright orange shaft on the water still followed me as I walked, until the sun rose to hide behind the first cloud, then disappeared as suddenly as it appeared. The sun then began its next function; to warm the new day. How could I have missed this spectacle for three straight mornings?

Harriet sat in her chair, reading her newspaper, smoking a cigarette as usual. "Morning, dummy," she said.

I wanted to be nice to her but couldn't get past her not warning me about the party kids. Although, in fairness, I probably wouldn't have believed her. She doesn't deserve any fairness from me. I looked her way but didn't answer.

I spent the early afternoon walking uptown, looking in store windows, and sitting in a small park, watching people and their pets. I bought some postcards, then wondered why. I didn't have anyone to send them to; no one who would want to keep track of my travels; no one waiting for me to come back. No one knows or cares I'm here.

After a while, I felt the tug of the ocean. I walked down the beach farther than before and found a park with hiking trails. One trail passed through trees and shrubs along the sand and turned inward through a large stand of trees. It offered a pleasant, cool shade when the sun was highest. The park also had a pier that extended into the ocean quite a ways. I spent my day alternating between soaking in the sun at the end of the pier and walking in the shade of the trees.

I stayed until dusk then walked back to the cabin. The beach party was again in full swing, but no one offered an invitation. Once was enough for me and they knew I wouldn't be the life of their party ever again.

Weekday parties don't last late into the night, so once the noise began to die, I opened a cabin window and fell asleep to the gentle sound of waves crashing against the sand.

I awoke once more, well before dawn, fixed a small breakfast and walked to the water's edge to greet another day.

Today was to be my last. Harriet made a point to tell me that if I wasn't out by ten, she would charge me for another day. "Yain't stayin' here for free, dummy," she had growled.

I assured her I would leave before her deadline and even if I were to stay longer, it wouldn't be in one of her cabins. I loaded my stuff in the Chevy and moved it to public parking before leaving for the beach.

As I sat watching God's light show here for the last time, it dawned on me that I did not have a new destination. I still had no desire to return to Kitty's. I had made a choice that was best for both of us. I had given up the hope of ever finding Janie. I had given up having a home or ever finding any happiness.

The ocean offered me a calmness I hadn't felt for a while, but the people here weren't nice. If I was drawn by the water, it wasn't this water. I had seen the sunrise over the ocean. I would like to see a sunset over the ocean too. I'll go to California to watch the sunset.

But first, I wanted to make the most of my last day here.

As I pulled on my new swimming trunks, I regretted a little taking the shirt back to Janice. If I still had it, I would wear it today; finish my last day here by sitting close to the party group with it on. But there wasn't any point. They knew and I knew they had made a fool of me. They knew and I knew I was a better person than any of them.

I found an empty coffee can on the shelf in the cabin and took it to the beach to fill it with shells. I walked to the pier under a brightening sky to watch my last beach sunrise from the end, high above the water. A young couple with their arms around each other's waists sat in the chairs beside me. They came equipped with a blanket and soon were huddled together against the cool breeze. Only their faces were visible. They caught one of my gazes of envy and simply smiled; happiness shone in their eyes.

The three of us sat and watched the sun break the horizon with an orange sliver, then watched as the sliver turned to a brilliant yellow ball, tinging the gray clouds orange and red and yellow. Then it began to warm the cool morning air. Each sunrise is different but spectacular as you view it. Why aren't more people here to watch?

It didn't take long to fill my coffee can. I soon discovered every shell was unique and pretty in its way, much like sunrises. I saw no point in filling the can with shells that held no special meaning. I spread them on the beach, sorted out the nicest four, stuffed them in my pocket, and left the rest for the shell collectors that would follow. I imagined frolicking kids walking this beach years from now, picking up pretty shells, showing them to their parents and giggling.

Chapter 19

*T*he heat from the afternoon sun told me it was time to leave. I could probably still rent a cabin somewhere else for a few more days or weeks, but spectacular sunrises were not enough to keep me here. I began my slow walk to my Chevy in the parking lot to begin the drive to California. With my four favorite shells wrapped in a handkerchief lying on the seat beside me, I started toward a sunset on a beach in California. As the sun began to set behind me, I drove toward Charleston to spend my night in Wide Awake again.

I rose to a dark, dreary day. It was cold, the wind was blowing hard out of the north and almost ripped the door from my hand as I opened it. No sunrise to watch today; no sand between my toes or shells to collect. I was only a little more than two hours from the beach.

I sat on the edge of the bed and wondered if going west was a mistake. I sat thinking until finally I got up and loaded my stuff in the Chevy. I ate breakfast at a little biscuit shop next door. Then, with a full stomach and full gas tank, I turned onto the highway and started west toward a sunset over a sandy beach.

Soon I was back in the hills of South Carolina, passing through one small town after another; one small farm after another tucked at the far end of the valleys. Back to the type of land I was comfortable in. By evening, I found a motor court in a little town called Opelika in Alabama and stopped for the night. A huge man sauntered out front when I drove up. He wore a flannel shirt with a torn sleeve under his bib overalls; sort of like Ray used to. His cap lay back on his head so far I wondered why it didn't fall off; the bill was all smashed and crooked like it had been stomped by a herd of cows. He was popping some little nuts in his mouth as he spoke, "Burly's the name, son. What's yours?" he asked.

"Folks call me Rusty," I answered.

"Yup, fits you just like mine fits me, I reckon. You stayin' a spell or just passin' through?" he asked. Then, before I could answer, he held out a bag.

"Have yerself a handful o' nuts."

"Just for one night, Burly. I'm traveling. I saw a sunrise from the beach in South Carolina. Now I'm headed to California. I want to see a sunset on the beach there too. What kind of nuts are these?" I answered while he poured me a handful of nuts.

"They's boiled peanuts. Pretty tasty, don'tcha think?

"They're alright, I guess," I answered.

"Alright! They's a whole lot better 'n just alright," he bellowed and laughed. "Lotta people from up north don't like them right off, say they's a 'quired taste, whatever that means. Y'all from up north, Rusty?"

"Sort of. I was born in Iowa, but I haven't been there for a long time," I told him.

"You're lookin' kinda' puny there, boy, like you need some grub. Go on up there to Archie's, right up there on the corner. Tell him Burly sent ya. He'll fill ya up," Burly said, still with the big grin. "Make sure you get a piece of Archie's famous pecan pie. Folks come to town from all over, just for a slice. Come on back after, we'll sit an jaw a spell. Don't think I ever met no Iowegian before," he said. I decided to follow his instructions. I was pretty hungry after all.

"Nelly, fetch up a Burly special. We got us a visitor in the house," Archie called to the kitchen as soon as I told him Burly sent me. "Where y'all from, son?"

"Up north," I answered.

"Just 'up north?' that's all ya got? Folks must not talk much 'up north'."

"Burly's up," came the call from the kitchen.

In mere seconds, Archie put a huge plate of fried chicken, okra, and grits all covered with white gravy, and a steaming biscuit pushed down on the top. It looked like a picture of a volcano I had seen in a book once.

"Here ya go, son. Eat up, but save some room for a slice of pecan pie. Sweet tea or water?"

"Water."

"Yup, you's from up north alright. Don't understand why you Northern-ers ain't got a taste for sweet tea," he grinned.

I was glad I had walked up from Burly's. I couldn't have forced my stuffed belly under the steering wheel of the Chevy. "Breakfast at six," Archie called, as the screen door latched behind me.

Burly was waiting as I walked up the steps, "Pull yerself up a chair, take a load off," he said.

I didn't feel much like talking but I sat anyway. Turned out, talkin' was just an expression for Burly. He meant listening, because he did all the talking. I silently learned all about Burly and about Burly's family, Opelika, how to plant peanuts, how to pick peanuts, the best way to boil peanuts, and the War. Folks down here were still fighting the War, which is how they refer to the Civil War. The War had ended seventy years ago. It was the War to end all wars to the South. They had fought and lost it but were still in denial. Down here, as far as they were concerned, it wasn't over yet. It surprised me that he showed no animosity to me, a Northern-er. Somehow, he didn't think of me as the enemy.

"I need to get some sleep, Burly. I'll be off early in the morning," I said.

"Naw, ya need to spend the day. See the town. We got us a purty town here. Y'all could like it here if ya had a mind to. Go on, git some rest, be seein' ya in the mornin'," he said as I forced my food-heavy, tired-to-the-bone body out of the chair.

"Night, then," I said.

I rose early, although I missed the sunrise. Somehow, it didn't seem worth the effort; it wouldn't compare to yesterday's on the beach. Burly stood in the drive.

"Got some biscuits and gravy if you want. Marge is cleaning the rooms; it's her turn since I closed last night. Come on, have a sit. Have a cup of Marge's coffee. It'll wake ya up or kill ya," he laughed, but still didn't stop talking.

"Take me for a ride in that fancy car and I'll show you the sights. I told Marge you'd probably be stayin' another day. Lot's to see an' do here."

We sat–first at his kitchen table– then on the porch drinking the strongest coffee I had ever tasted. He held up his cup for a toast. "Told ya. Feel like ya kin whip the world now, don't ya? I always told Marge, if the boys coulda all had yer coffee ever morning, we'd a beat them Yanks," he laughed, but I could already feel the truth in his words. I was wide awake now.

We drove around all morning in my car. His jabber never stopped.

"Got my first kiss right there under that lamppost. Weren't Marge neither. My uncle used to have a feed store right here on this corner, but it burnt down. Little brother Ned fell off a horse down that lane a piece; never was the same after. Pa, he done shot the horse. Them Mitchell girls lived over there. They was always good for a fun time, if'n ya get my drift? This little house is where I was born. All my brothers and sisters too, eleven of us, all told."

It was almost noon when we got back to the motor lodge. This morning, listening to Burly had been nice. I envied him; proud of his town and content with his life. He didn't have the emptiness inside I felt.

"I'm going to move on, Burly. I like your town. Like it a lot, but it's time for me to go," I said.

He gave me a bag with a couple of biscuits, some apples and bananas, and a huge sack of boiled peanuts, "Ain't gonna' have 'em where yer goin'," he said. I watched in the mirror as he stood in the middle of the road, waving like he was seeing a son off to war, knowing he would never see him again.

On the road to Jackson I learned that boiled peanuts are an acquired taste, and it would take time to acquire it. At first, I ate them one after another, leaving a trail of peanut hulls on the highway. But after a day of driving in the heat, eating peanuts, and drinking water non-stop, I closed the bag and put it in the trunk at a gas stop. The heat and humidity in Mississippi and Alabama seemed to boil the mixture in my gut. On the edge of Jackson I found another motor lodge and stopped for the night. The room was hot and stuffy, so I opened the windows and front door and sat in the lounge chair out front with a glass of unsweetened tea to watch the cars drive by. I was paying more attention to the rumbling in my stomach than the street but caught a glimpse of a curly blonde-haired girl riding past in a car.

"Janie!" I yelled as I jumped to my feet.

I ran for my car to follow. But it didn't start right away. In my haste, I flooded it and had to crank the motor for what seemed like an hour before it would clear out and start. By the time I made it to the street, Janie's car was out of sight. I followed her route to the edge of town, but she was gone. I couldn't see taillights ahead on the road, so I turned around, drove back to town, and began to search, street by street. After a stressful thirty minutes, I saw the car in front of a grocery. I stopped in the street for a few moments until I was sure it was empty, then I parked a few spaces away. I walked to the front of the store and peered in the windows. She was nowhere in sight, so I sat on the bench in front to wait and watch.

Needing to know finally got the best of me, so I went in. People started giving me curious looks as I hurried up one aisle and down another, obviously not shopping for groceries.

She stood with a man about twice her age looking at the bread selection. Is that really her? Is that her boyfriend? Maybe she's married. If I could only hear her voice, then I would know.

"Excuse me," I stammered. "I am looking for oatmeal, I thought it would be here with the bread. Do you know where I can find it?" I asked.

"I think it's two aisles over with the cereal," the man answered.

Damn–he spoke instead of her! She sure looks like Janie, but she didn't look up when I asked. How can I get her to say something?

"Thanks," I said. Then blurted, "Folks call me Rusty," hoping to get some type of reaction, but she still didn't speak, only looked at me and smiled.

I stood for several uncomfortable moments until I finally had to walk away. I found the oatmeal and unfortunately, they only had the big cans. Now, carrying a can of oatmeal under my arm, I followed them through the store. Everyone was now watching me. Everyone but Janie. Eventually, they carried their goods to the check-out. I followed, but a rude old woman with a cartload of groceries squeezed between them and me. "Hi, Abby, did you and Micky find everything you needed?" the checkout lady asked.

I crowded the old woman, straining to hear her answer.

"Yup, just came in for a loaf of bread but ended up with an armload. Y'all know how it goes, don'tcha?"

From the first word, I knew it wasn't her. It couldn't be. I hadn't heard Janie's voice for years, but I could tell. I couldn't stand there and just watch her, the disappointment took the strength from my legs. I set the can of oatmeal on the counter and left. People were still gawking at me as I got in my car, but I didn't care.

I slowly drove back to the motel, collapsed in the lounge chair, leaned forward, and held my head in my hands.

How stupid to think that down here in the middle of Mississippi I would see my sister driving past me in an automobile. Things just don't work that way. Things that are too good to be true hardly ever happen and they sure never happen to me. Besides, the girl was only about twelve-years-old. Janie would be nineteen by now.

After dark I went inside and lay in the bed, staring at the ceiling. Thinking, wondering, but not sleeping.

Chapter 20

*F*or the second morning in a row, the sun woke me. Uncharacteristically, I lay on the bed for quite some time before forcing my feet to the floor. Seeing a sunset over the ocean didn't seem so important anymore, but I didn't have anything else, so I ate breakfast, loaded the car, and started driving.

It is hard to tell much difference between Alabama, Mississippi, and Louisiana–it's all just flat and a lot of trees there. What hills there are aren't very big or very steep. I drove all day, with the remainder of the peanuts locked in the trunk.

I knew Dallas was a big city. I didn't want to drive through in the evening and I didn't want to stop there for the night, so I found a motor lodge in Longview, Texas to spend the night. Since my hopes had been dashed last night when I thought I saw Janie, I kept to myself. I paid the lady in the office without even learning her name. I found a sandwich shop close by and ordered dinner, ham, and fried potatoes, by asking the waitress for a #2 on the menu. I took my tea refill, returned to the cabin, closed the door, sat in the chair, and stared at the wall.

I ordered breakfast at the same place, the same way. "I'd like a #3." Once I finished, I had the Chevy filled with gas, the oil and water checked, and began a new day. I hoped to get through Dallas without stopping for anything. Before leaving, I studied my map and realized I could go around Dallas in about the same amount of driving time. I had done all that worrying for nothing.

Yesterday I noticed the trees were changing; big tall green trees began giving way to smaller, scraggly looking ones. Green pastures were becoming brown. North of Dallas, the land began to look more and more like a desert. The ground was a dirty red color. Fields were desolate; the wheat had been picked leaving only the brown stalks. Cattle grazed in scrub grass that looked like it didn't have any nourishment.

I drove all day without seeing any water. There were no lakes, no streams with water flowing, not even any puddles.

When I crossed a bridge and looked down, I saw only dry riverbed. That evening, when I got to Childress, Texas, I had little doubt this country was not a place for me.

I found another motor lodge; they were beginning to look all the same. This one was run by a nice old couple, Joe and Ellie. "Where y'all from?" Ellie asked as I walked into the little office. She wore a print dress and a turquoise necklace with a big silver pendant. The pendant had three silver feathers, and each had some bright red yarn wrapped around it.

"Well, I guess I'm from all over," I answered. Her question caught me off-guard.

"Well then, where y'all goin'?" she asked.

"I'm going to California, see a sunset," I said.

"Seems like a lot of trouble, just to see a sunset. There's no need to go all that way; we got some mighty fine sunsets right here. Just fix yourself a snack, drive out of town a couple of miles, park along the road, and sit. Sunset will come along soon enough. We got some big ones out here, guaranteed to please. Me and Joe been doin' it together for almost fifty years, and we ain't tired of 'em yet." she grinned.

Joe came from the side door. He towered over me; must have been six-five at least. He had a vest on over his big barrel chest. It had been years, if ever, since he had been able to button it. Ellie walked over next to Joe. He reached around her waist, picked her up with one arm, and kissed her on top of her head. They stood there smiling, him in his old sweat-worn cowboy hat, and both with silver-studded fancy boots they had obviously been wearing for a long time. Joe looked at me, scratched his long gray beard, and smiled. "Got a little growth started there on yer face, son. Been workin' it long?"

I smiled back.

"Well, ya got a good start anyway. Keep at it. Mine was red like yours once. Reckon all them long days on the ranch caused the sun to bleach it out. Name's Joe, nobody calls me that. Round here, everybody calls me Big'un," he smiled, extending his hand to shake.

My hand almost disappeared in his. He squeezed a little; his big warm grip could have broken every bone in my hand.

"My real name is Russell, but most folks call me Rusty, what with my red beard," I told him.

"Good name, I like it. You fixin' to stay around? I can get you a job doin' most anything if you want. Lots of work around here, most of the young 'uns went off to fight the Germans and Japs. This sure is a purty place to live if yer lookin' for one. Me and Ellie been here in Childress since we was kids. Been married almost that long too," Joe said.

Ellie was right. That evening, I took a mug of tea and some crackers to the edge of town, leaned on the hood of the Chevy, and saw one of the prettiest sunsets ever–prettiest without water anyway.

Joe's offer was tempting. I was starting to run out of money, but the thought of staying here, in a land with no trees and no water, wouldn't do. Maybe Amarillo will be a better place to stop for a while.

The sunrise here was pretty too, but I came back to the cabin planning to move on. I put my stuff in the Chevy and said goodbye. Ellie wrapped a piece of cake and put it in a bag for me. Joe grabbed my hand. "Childress could use a nice young man like you," he said, smiling down at me, squeezing again.

I thought–but not out loud–I'll bet there are a lot of people with sore hands in Childress.

It only took about three hours to get to Amarillo. By noon, I was driving around the city, looking. Most yards were dirt and rock. The streets were all dusty. Cars didn't look like they had ever been washed. It was worse than Childress, with no trees of any size and the only green anywhere was something that had been painted. The decision to drive on from here was easy. I would make it to Albuquerque with the money I had left, but there I was going to have to find work before I could go on. The gas station attendant in Albuquerque was more worried about my water supply than my gas. "Got a water jug?" he asked.

I said yes and showed him my jug. "Man, that two-gallon jug ain't big enough. Besides, it's not even full. People die out there just because their car died or they had a flat tire. I'm gonna fill that jug and git you another."

"I don't need a second jug and I can't afford to buy one," I told him.

"Y'all's takin' a second jug. I'm giving you one whether you want it or not. I ain't having your death burning my conscience," he answered.

He was a big man and determined. I didn't want to make him mad so I took the extra jug, just so I would satisfy him.

The road from Amarillo to Albuquerque was like nothing I'd ever seen before. I drove miles and miles in stifling heat, not meeting any cars, not seeing any houses, not seeing anything. Not even any animals. Fifteen to thirty minutes passed between meeting cars and I didn't see any going in my direction, either in front or behind me. I wanted to drive faster, to get this over with, but I didn't dare. My life depended on this old Chevy, the gas in its tank, the tires on the road, and the water in the back seat. We were in this together. I drove for over three hours before getting to Santa Rosa. I stopped and had the water and oil checked and filled up with gas.

The guy in Amarillo was right; a person could easily die out here.

I arrived in Albuquerque late in the evening. The old Chevy had lost its enthusiasm for the highway and I had too. The highways of New Mexico were long, lonely, and hot. I remembered the heat of Memphis, how hot it got in Kitty's on those long days in August. But Texas and New Mexico were different. The heat here made it hard to breathe. It came down from the sky and up from the ground. Neither shade nor breeze helped; there was no escape.

The thought of staying a couple of months in Albuquerque to earn some money before heading on toward California for a sunset no longer appealed to me. I had seen the Atlantic sunrises and was satisfied. I guess the only real reason to see the Pacific was to be able to tell that I had seen both, but I didn't have anyone to tell, so what was the point?

It didn't take me long to feel the need to move on from Albuquerque. The sun beat down within minutes after appearing from below the east horizon. The burning lasted well after it had set below the west. Buildings here were brown, streets were brown, people were brown, the entire landscape was brown. Even cars were brown from all the dust raised by the constant wind.

I missed the green. Green grass, green trees, green fields. I smiled at the thought of green tea. The west was not the place for me. I was tired, lonesome, and homesick. But I didn't have a home to go to.

Chapter 21

I decided to give up on California. I no longer felt the need to see the ocean and I sure didn't want to drive through more desert to get there. I didn't even want to drive anymore.

I found a used car dealer on Third Avenue, close to the railroad tracks. He was willing to buy my Chevy for a fair price. "I'd like to give you more, but them tires are shot," he said. "I'm going to have to come up with new ones somehow before I can sell it."

I took everything I owned out of the back, except the boiled peanuts, walked to the depot, looked at the train schedule, bought a ticket to Ft. Madison, Iowa, and sat on a bench in the lobby to wait. I wanted to see the home place again. I wanted to look at Mama's and Grandpa Red's graves,.Moose's, too.

Most of all, I needed to look for Janie again.

The conductor looked at me as I boarded. "That all you got, son?"

"Yes, sir. Everything I have is in my bag."

"You can clean up in the restroom if you'd like," he said.

I had been in the heat for the last two days. I guess he could tell.

This was my first time on a train. I really liked it. I could get up and walk around, look out the windows or close my eyes and rest, all while it was moving. It even had a place where I could eat. The bathrooms were small, but that didn't matter; they were clean. It was nice just getting to use one when I needed it. It felt good to be able to see the scenery outside without having to watch the highway. I should have tried this sooner.

There wasn't much I could see, though.

I boarded the train in the evening and by the time I got settled, the sun was beginning to disappear behind the mountains. The colors in the sky rivaled those in South Carolina, but they didn't last long. The sun disappeared long before the colors had run their full gamut. I watched until the last bit of blue turned gray, then settled into my seat and closed my eyes. Almost instantly the rocking and clickity-click of the wheels lulled me to sleep.

My bleary eyes opened to the same stark scenery. The vistas of Southeast Colorado rival those in Texas and New Mexico–desolate. I looked at the same rock, cactus, rocky soil, and tumbleweeds of the desert. But they soon gave way to the endless miles of wheat fields, pasture, and tumbleweeds of southwest Kansas.

I went to the dining car, found a seat in a corner alone, ate a small breakfast, and drank a second, then a third cup of coffee before returning to my seat. A lady across from me was now fussing with an unruly little boy.

She looked a little like Kitty, only with a child. That could be my son if I had stayed. The thought of what my life could have been flashed through my mind. It scared me to think of what I may have missed. I felt a deep envy and emptiness. Wouldn't it be wonderful to have a wife and child?

I began to change my mind about riding the train. Yes, the train had dining and bathroom facilities; but in a car, I can stop, get out and breathe fresh air whenever I want. And I can be alone when I need to be.

With nothing to see but small towns with big grain elevators, I napped on and off all afternoon. My naps were restless, frequently interrupted by the child across from me, still fussing. The thought of seeing the farm after so long made me nervous. I wondered if it would look the same. Mr. Webster is probably taking good care of it. I wonder if he has fixed the fence next to the barn. It will be good to see old Sam again. I wonder if he will recognize me.

As I sat gazing, thinking, I noticed the world outside was gradually turning greener. Fields now had fences. Fence rows had cedar and hedge trees. Farms now had grass in the water runoffs. Houses had yards again. Houses were closer together. Towns got closer together, and bigger. The porter yelled, "Kansas City, twenty minutes. Next stop, Kansas City." I hurried to a dome car to see.

We passed through neighborhoods where grown-ups were sitting on porches or leaning against their cars watching kids playing ball in the streets. They stopped their game long enough to pump their arms, a signal to ask the engineer to blow his whistle. He obliged with a long shrill blast that set them jumping and laughing.

"Kansas City. Watch your step folks, Kansas City. We'll be here twenty minutes if you want to stretch your legs. Don't get too far, easy to get lost, engineer'll blow the whistle 'fore we leave. But if you ain't here, we'll be leavin' without you," the porter said.

I walked around in the depot for a while but didn't dare leave the building. The thought of being lost in a huge city because I missed the train scared me. I was back on the train long before he called, "All aboard."

The last bit of blue sky was turning gray as we began to pick up speed on the outskirts of the city. So, with nothing more to see but lights in the black countryside, I climbed down from the dome car and returned to my seat. "Blankets, anyone need a blanket?" our porter asked, as he walked through the car. I took one, pulled it up around my neck, scrunched against the window, closed my eyes, and tried to get comfortable.

"Ft. Madison, sir."

My bleary eyes opened to a porter standing over me.

"Ft. Madison, sir, your stop. Sir, time to get off," he repeated.

I stood on the platform in the foggy darkness, watching the light on the rear of the train until it disappeared into the fog from a river, leaving me holding my bag. Alone.

Chapter 22

A flashing red light shone through the fog from the city above. It was the only sign of life in this sleeping river town. I slung my bag over my shoulder and trudged across the tracks, up the hill, and across the street. An OPEN sign clung to the pole outside a tiny diner. In the dimly lit interior, I could see a woman leaning against the bar, reading a paper. All the stools were vacant. I pushed the rickety door open and stepped inside. Without looking up, she asked, "Coffee?"

"Yes, please," I answered.

I chose the end stool, the farthest from the door, laid my bag against the wall, and sat. A steaming cup was sitting on the counter before I could land. There were eight stools along one wall, three booths along the other. The walls had photos of men in uniform, pictures of boats, and posters of events all long past. It wasn't fancy, but it smelled good. It reminded me of Sadie at the Fine's Creek Store.

"Would you like to see a menu?" She stood over me with a cigarette hanging from the corner of her mouth. She was short with short brown hair, wearing a headscarf that served as a hair net. The white apron she wore over a pair of blue jeans and a flannel shirt was covered with stains. I wondered how long since it was last washed.

"Just coffee, I guess," I said.

"Look at the menu. Tell me what you want. Nobody here but you and me. It's been a slow night. I'll fix you up. I could use someone to talk to," she said, without expression.

"Ok, but I don't much care," I said, looking down at the menu.

"Oh, what the hell, one special coming up," she said. "How do you like your eggs?" she said, as she turned toward the grill in the back.

She was gone before I could answer.

I leaned against the wall and watched as she moved, almost with grace, around her kitchen. It was a well-practiced routine done almost without thought. In minutes, she flopped a plate–heaped with hash browns covered with gravy, three sunny-side-up eggs, two big sausage links, and two steaming biscuits–in front of me. Then she leaned forward, propped her elbows on the bar, and smiled. "Where you headed, stranger?"

"Stockport."

"What are you going there for?" she asked.

"I lived there once," I answered.

"Not many people out this time a night. You must have just got off the train? Stockport is a ways off. How are you getting there if you don't have a car?" she asked.

"It's not that far, I looked on a map. I'll walk there in the morning," I said.

"I can get you a ride if you want. My brother works the Peavine. It's a local train. It leaves every morning about five, goes to the Eldon Turn and comes back late afternoon. It goes right through Stockport. Leaves in about an hour if you want?" she said. "It's not a passenger train but they will let people ride sometimes. It leaves from the other end of town. They'll let you just hop on if you want."

"I don't want to be any bother," I answered.

"It isn't any bother. Ask for Johnny–he's my brother. Tell him Judy sent you. There'll be a pot brewing and he likes to talk. Me too, I guess. Good luck to you. Come back by and say hi sometime."

She pushed a couple of sandwiches in my pack as I swung it over my shoulder again, then handed me a thermos with a lid on it. I tried to refuse, but she said, "Give it to Johnny when it's empty, he'll give it back to me."

"Sixteenth and Avenue H. That's Avenue H you just crossed. Just step outside the door and turn right. It's only ten blocks; you can't miss it. There's a little shack on the corner. They'll be in it," she said as I pushed on the door to leave.

"Hey, I almost forgot, what's your handle?" she asked as I was about to step outside.

"My handle?"

"Yeah, what do you go by; what's your name?"

"Folks call me Rusty," I answered.

"Well, get a move on then. Nice to meet you, Rusty. Tell Johnny, I said, 'Hi.'"

I set off into the darkness to find a train with a shack beside it, hopefully with a light.

"What's your name, Bud?"

"Folks call me Rusty. Judy sent me. Are you Johnny?"

"Yup, that'd be me. Where are you going?"

"Stockport."

"Well, this is your lucky day, Rusty. Just so happens we go right through there. Got family there?"

"Uh, no. Used to, but not anymore."

Johnny showed me into the caboose, poured me a cup of coffee, and pointed to a bench along the wall. "Hold on to your cup; ride gets a little rough sometimes," he said.

We chugged up the hill and out of town. Soon wew were rolling along in the dark about forty miles an hour. Our first stop was in West Point, where the crew switched out some full grain cars and left empties. Then we motored on to St. Paul to leave some empties at the elevator. At Houghton, we had to stop on the edge of town because there was a tractor parked too close to the tracks. Johnny, his helper, and I climbed off the train to see if we could move the tractor. It wouldn't start and we couldn't push it, so we all walked into town to the café. We didn't find who we were looking for, so we walked on to the feed store to find someone who knew someone who knew the owner so he could come move it. Apparently, they knew who owned the tractor and this had happened before.

I was already nervous and we were wasting time. It had been about fifteen years since I left the farm and it was driving me crazy to be this close and not seem to be able to get any closer.

We finally found the guy they were looking for. He was sleeping in a chair in the back of the feed store. He wasn't too happy about getting roused from his sleep, but grudgingly, he followed us back to the train and moved his tractor out of our way. Then he climbed in the caboose and flopped on the bench.

Apparently, this was routine, hauling him back to town. Johnny apologized for all the time we were taking. I heard him tell the engineer, "Let's skip Hillsboro, we can pick it up on the way back."

Then he turned to me and called, "Stockport, main street, next stop," like he was the conductor on a large passenger train.

As I stepped off the train and onto the street, Johnny said, "If you need a ride back, just be standing here about five this evening. We'll be watching for you." He was still standing on the back platform waving as the train disappeared toward Birmingham and the Eldon turnaround.

For the second time in a few hours, I stood with my bag and watched as the light of a train disappeared into the distance. Slowly, I walked to the corner of Main and Cedar to see my old friend, Stockport.

A new bank had replaced the livery stable. On the opposite corner stood a gas station in place of the blacksmith shop. I walked on to where the school stood; it was now closed and the windows were boarded up. A cafe stood where the church had been, and a beauty parlor was now in the front of Mrs. Johnson's house. The feedstore was gone; an empty lot was all that remained.

I walked on to Mr. Kerr's General Store. A closed sign hung in the door behind a broken window. The roof over the porch was drooping. The front windows were boarded. I rubbed the window in the door with my sleeve and peered in. I wished I hadn't. The inside had been ransacked, shelves ripped off the walls, display cases dumped, pictures were broken and trash was scattered everywhere.

I left Stockport wishing I hadn't come. Wishing Johnny's train had let me off at the road on the far side of town where my old path home started. From now on, I would no longer remember Stockport as it once was, but as it is now. If I could only unsee what I had just seen.

I walked the road to our old place on the Cedar. The dirt was covered with gravel now. At the intersection, I left the road and walked the path along the fence row, just like I used to.

The path that I had walked so many times before with Mama and Janie was all grown up in weeds and bushes. I wondered if anyone had walked it since my last time.

I slowed as I approached the bluff overlooking my home place. At the base, I stopped, Do I really need to do this? I stood, hopeful, but fearing what I might see.

Instinctively, I dropped to the ground and crawled to the edge of the bluff and peered over the edge. The house was gone. Burned. Nothing but the chimney stood. The cookstove was all that remained. It sat covered with ash against the rock foundation. The barn roof had caved in, but the walls still stood; twisted and drooping. It looked like it could collapse any minute. The chicken coop and storage shed both had fallen; trees were growing through the remains of their roofs. Our fields were overgrown in weeds, I couldn't see any of our fences.

I walked down to the ford and crossed the creek, then stood in front of the burned-out remains of what once had been my home. I walked through the doorway and stood where Mama's chair used to rock. Silently, I looked around as tears began to form. The only sounds I heard were the barn door creaking as it swung in the breeze and me sobbing. The yard had been washed away by a flood, probably more than one. I went to Moose's boulder, crawled on it, and looked at the water. I thought about skipping rocks like I had years ago but couldn't bring myself to even pick one up.

Mama's and Moose's graves were covered with brush. I had to dig to find Grandpa Red's marker. I spent the afternoon pulling weeds and cleaning their headstones. Then, in the evening, I walked back across the creek andclimbed up the hill to spend the night.

I didn't sleep much. I cried mostly, wished I hadn't come, but knew I had to.

In the morning, I walked back down, crossed my footbridge, and walked up the hill to see Mr. Webster.

His house sat empty. Some scaffolding still stood around the outside. Poor Mrs. Webster, she never got to live in her dream house. The wood barn was empty. The stacks of oak, walnut, and sycamore he had cut to sell or use for the house were gone. The wood shorts and all the firewood were gone. I found the stool I used to sit on while I watched the sawmill do its magic. It lay on its side, one of the legs broken.

This all seemed like a dream now. Like Mr. and Mrs. Webster had never lived here. Like Mama and Janie and Moose had never been. Like I was the only person in the whole world.

I found the money Mr. Webster had hidden in the cellar. After Mama died, and I was struggling to work the farm alone, go to school and take care of Janie, he had told me he put some money aside for me.

"Rusty, I put some money in a fruit jar. It's in the root cellar. If things ever get tough and I am not around to help, use the money the best you can," he had said.

I stuffed the bills in my pocket and started toward town. I needed to look for Janie one last time.

The cop kept his hand on his pistol as he answered my questions. Then, when he finally realized that I only wanted help, he gave me directions to the courthouse where records were now kept.

"Ask to see the County Recorder. She will be the person who will be able to help you," he said.

The placard on her desk told me her name was Blanche. With a look of apprehension, maybe pity, she asked, "How can I help you?"

It had been many years since I had last been to Fairfield. Now, no longer a boy, I was not afraid to tell people about my background. With no shame or hesitation, I told her about the happenings all those years ago. She was struck by all that I had endured and was eager to do all she could for me. Blanche opened every file she thought might possibly have any information about Janie in it. Soon, the desk, the chairs, and even the floor were littered with papers. We spent the afternoon looking through information, hoping to find some hint of Janie's abduction. We went over everything, some more than once.

Finally, she looked at me in despair and said, "We've been through everything I can think of, Rusty. I don't know where else to look. It's getting late and I have to close for the day, but if you'll come back tomorrow, well, maybe then we can find something somewhere. I'm sure we will."

The next morning, she was already in her office when I got there. More files lay in piles on the floor. Her hair was a mess and she wore the same dress and blouse as the day before. I knew she had been here all night.

Today's search didn't find anything new. She looked up with tears in her eyes. "Rusty, I'm so sorry, there just isn't anything here. Nothing. Maybe your sister's birth was never registered. They used to do that. When babies were born at home, the doctor was supposed to give birth information to the state, but it didn't always happen. If you could find a family Bible. Parents used to record personal information like births, deaths, and weddings. Maybe neighbors could help?" Blanche said.

"I had Mama's Bible years ago, but I lost it," I told her. I looked at the floor, "There aren't any neighbors."

"I am so sorry, Rusty. I can't think of anywhere else to look."

We sat silently until the first morning customers began to come in.

"I will keep looking. I'll find something, I know I will. When I do, I'll get in touch with you. Where will you be?" she asked.

This was my last hope. I rose to leave. "I don't know where I will be. I'll check with you occasionally," I said. I knew she would keep looking. I knew she would probably never find anything. I knew I wouldn't come back.

She grabbed my arm as I turned to leave and hugged me, tears streamed down our cheeks, "You don't have to go. You can stay here with me, I'll find you a place. There are jobs here, I can help you find one. Maybe somebody in town knows something. There's always hope!" she said.

There wasn't any hope now; I knew it. This was my last try. I couldn't deal with the torment of not knowing anymore. She knew I was lying when I told her I would check back.

I knew I would never see Janie again.

Chapter 23

I struggled to push the Courthouse door open. I didn't remember pulling this hard when I came in. I held it open for a minute to let a young couple with a baby enter. Then, I let it close. It slammed behind me with a big thud. I felt all my life disappear when I heard it latch. I hesitated for a moment, looked around the lawn and then to the sky. The sun had fallen behind a dark cloud and the wind was beginning to blow.

I pulled my jacket up around my neck and walked down the steps to the sidewalk. On the street, I walked mindlessly through traffic and followed an alley to the downtown square. A bench under a huge oak tree caught my eye. I sat.

I watched people of every description walk by. All seemed to have a destination. I watched as some got in their cars and drove away, some crossed the street and entered stores, others found a bench and watched their children play. A sign on the south side of the square caught my eye. Under the Leggett Hotel sign, I saw the words BUS STOP.

At the ticket office, I asked the ticket agent for a ticket to Hidden Spring, Missouri. He searched his log for a minute, then said, "Rogersville is as close as I can get you, son."

The bus was almost empty when I got on. I found a seat close to the back, next to a window so I could be alone. Several people got on in Ottumwa, a few more in Bloomfield. A stop in Lancaster, then one in Kirksville filled all but a few seats. A lady with two little children sat across from me. A young couple, obviously in love, sat just in front.

I sat quietly, careful not to make eye contact with anyone. Most of the time, I stared vacantly out the window. I looked at the trees and fields, the buildings, and the hills without really seeing. My mind raced first one direction, then another. I couldn't focus. I tried to look away from the couple in front, but it wasn't possible. Why them? Why not me? It's not fair!

Once the lady's kids fell asleep, she wanted to talk. I ignored her as best I could, but she needed to talk to a grown-up and I was the nearest one. She bombarded me with questions. "Where you from? Where you going? You got friends there? What do you do?"

Finally, after a deluge of questions that brought her few answers, she got the hint and stopped asking. But she couldn't remain silent. She began telling me about herself. "I'm going to see my husband. He's in the Army. I haven't seen him for almost a year. He's finally back in the states. He's never even seen our new baby."

I turned back to the window and fell into the fog of my thoughts. Gradually the countryside began to look familiar. We passed a town I had seen before. I recognized a farmhouse where a lady had given me some food. I saw a barn where I had spent a night in the haymow. One sight after another brought me back to that time.

That time when I first was alone.

Then I saw the field–the field where the trucker had stopped. I saw the spot–the exact spot where he attacked me and the hedgerow that I ran to and hid behind.

"Why are you crying, sir?" she asked, "Is it something I said?"

I turned away from the window and saw her pleading face. I opened my mouth to speak but nothing came out. I hid my face in my hands until the tears stopped.

Once I composed myself enough to function, I walked to the front of the bus and begged the driver to stop.

"Sorry, son, but we don't stop here," he said.

"Please, sir, just let me off. I need to get off here. If you go on, I'll walk back," I pleaded.

"I'm sorry son, the next stop is Rogersville and I'm running late. You are getting off there. It won't be much longer.

"Please sir, I have to get off. Please."

Reluctantly, he stopped in the middle of the road and opened the door. Then he frowned at me for the inconvenience as I stepped off.

The back window was filled with curious faces as I stood with my pack, engulfed in exhaust smoke, and watched as the bus disappeared.

I walked the highway to the corner where the new gas station sat; the one that took all Ray's business. It felt awkward, but I went in. I bought a candy bar and filled my water jug, then went back out and sat on the guard rail near the edge of the parking lot.

I walked back to the entrance to the field where the truck driver had stopped all those long years ago; then began my search for Mama's Bible. He must have thrown it out with my clothes as soon as he realized I left them. He had to be worried that I might report him. He wouldn't dare be caught with my stuff in his truck.

I walked the edge of the road to Ray and Miriam's General Store, paused to look, then forced myself to walk on. I needed to look for the Bible, then I would come back. I walked down the hill to the edge of Hidden Spring; then turned around and walked back on the other side of the road. I walked in the ditch to the field where the trucker had stopped. After several quiet moments, I walked the ditch on the other side toward the General Store.

I didn't find the Bible or any trace of any of the things I carried that day. All my desire, all my will, all my hope was gone. I had nothing left.

Suddenly...finally...I knew what I was going to do.

The hills seemed higher and the valleys deeper than before as I walked south toward Miriam and Ray's store. My pack hurt my shoulders and I could hardly put one foot in front of the other. I struggled to keep going.

Just below the crest of a hill, I stopped to sit on my pack for a while. I knew what lay ahead. My mind was racing as fast as the car that flew by me. Its driver smiled and waved as he sped past, going toward Hidden Spring. I was relieved that he didn't offer me a ride.

I stopped at the base of the hill below the church and the General Store, a store that for a short time had been my store. I had just walked past three times and had purposely not gone up to it. Each time, I had forced myself to look only at the ground, telling myself I was searching for the Bible.

This time I looked up as I climbed the hill. The church roof had collapsed. All the stained-glass windows were broken or stolen. Somehow, the steeple still stood, and the bell still hung in the tower.

I tried to force open the door, put my shoulder against it, and pushed with all my might, but it wouldn't budge. I fought my way through the weeds to get to a side window and peered through. It was dark inside. The tree next to the building was now so big it blocked out most of the light. I saw limbs, leaves and other debris inside, blown in from years of weather. The pews were rotting. The pulpit where the preacher had once stood had fallen over. It lay broken on the floor. Birds had built nests inside. They squawked at me, an invader, as they buzzed me while constantly flying in and out. The vacant feeling of the church drew my thoughts from me.

I crossed the road to the General Store.

Boards were broken on the porch. One corner of the roof had collapsed. Ray's sign was hanging by just one chain, eerily swaying in the breeze. The yard was now all weeds. Trash was scattered everywhere. Ray's old chair lay next to the fence, with an armrest gone. The crowns of both gas pumps were missing, stolen probably. The broken windows in the front door were boarded up. Our stove still sat in the middle of the floor with a coffee pot on top, like someone only needed to build the fire to brew a pot of coffee. Surprisingly, the chair I built was sitting on the porch, still the exact same distance from the wall for Ray to lean back and "conduct bi'ness." My *Rusty's Repair* sign was leaning against the wall, strangely clean and dust-free.

I tested the chair, then sat. I felt a sense of apprehension and reverence. It was always special when Ray allowed anyone to sit in his chair. "Rusty built me that chair," he would proudly say.

The fence around the garden still stood. The gate creaked when I opened it. I found myself standing in the middle of a briar patch. There were no longer any corn stalks, nothing remained of the bean patch. A few volunteer tomatoes had tried to claim a space, but they too were being choked by weeds, growing with no fear of the hoe.

My workshop looked the same. After all this time, it hadn't changed. My repairs were still evident. I stopped short of going in. I couldn't even force myself to look in the window.

To my astonishment, the flower garden was still there. Flowers of all types grew in a weed-free oasis. Miriam's bench, just as nice as the last time I had seen it, had a tablecloth neatly folded over one end.

Time seemed to pause as one memory after another flashed through my brain. Sadness, fear, disappointment, and emptiness crushed me. Any hope of happiness–or the anticipation for it–were gone now. I leaned back against the wall and thought, much as Ray must have all those years ago. My eyes fell on the steeple of the church. I wondered if Ray's eyes might have also.

I watched as an old hound dog appeared from the trees. He limped toward me with a painful, forlorn expression. His eyes had long ago lost their sparkle, the hair on his chin was now sprinkled with gray. He struggled up the step to the porch and brushed my leg as if to acknowledge me. Then he sighed as he collapsed on the porch floor. Air burst from his lungs.

I looked down at the pathetic creature. Once he had been someone's constant companion, now he was forgotten and alone. He lay there just waiting to die.

The more I looked at him, the more I saw the similarity.

We were somehow the same, but yet, we weren't really.

We were different; the old hound and me. He had to lay and wait for his end.

I didn't.

With renewed conviction, I went back to the garden, picked the two prettiest lilies I could find, walked back for a final look at the store, the church, and the hound. I started down the hill toward town.

As I got closer, I could see there was a crowd of people at the lake. Some were in the water. It looked like a ceremony.

I decided to wait until they finished before going on.

It took an excruciating amount of time. One at a time, they entered the water, did something I couldn't quite make out, then returned to the shore. I watched until finally, the entire group began climbing up the hill to a tent full of tables.

Once the beach was deserted, I walked to the water's edge, where I stood alone still holding the lilies. I felt the water lapping at my feet. I realized I was still wearing my boots. The pair I just bought in Amarillo.

It would be a shame to waste such good boots. I sat on the shore, unlaced them, took them off, placed them together on the sand, put a lily in each, and left them for a new owner.

The water hadn't seemed this cold ever before. My feet grew numb as I stood there, ankle-deep.

I began to move forward with the water first around my shins, then almost to my knees. I hesitated before taking another step. It was now above my knees and cold numbed my whole body. Thoughts raced through my brain. Thoughts of people and places. I thought about Miriam and Ray, Kitty, Grandpa Red, and Moose. Mostly though, I thought about Mama and Janie.

I continued deeper into the water, now up to my thighs, and hesitated again.

"Brother, you look like you could use a good meal," a voice called.

I moved again; the water was to my waist now.

"Brother, won't you come join us at our table?" the voice called again.

The interruption caused me to pause. I turned to look.

A young man, dressed in a long white robe, stood at the water's edge. "Brother, please come join us. We would love to share our meal," he implored.

I didn't move.

I tried, but I couldn't move.

He waded to where I stood, took my hand, and said, "My name is Brother Joseph. Won't you come join my friends and share our meal?"

My will would no longer force me deeper into the cold. My legs went limp.

I stumbled as he helped me from the lake and up the hill to the tent, where he found a seat for me.

"Please sit and enjoy our fellowship," he smiled.

My legs still were not capable of holding me up. I sank, trembling and dripping water, onto the bench. Instantly a smiling lady laid a plate heaped with fried chicken, green beans, and mashed potatoes smothered with gravy in front of me. Another put her hand on my shoulder and smiled as she set silverware and a glass of tea. A little girl with a beaming smile and sparkling eyes and carrying a basket of steaming biscuits approached. Hand to hand, a tub of butter passed toward me, each hand connected to a face with a warm expression. The eyes in the tent then bore down on me as I began to devour the food.

Brother Joseph rose from his chair and moved to the pulpit, much like the preacher must have in the old church at the top of the hill. Silence fell over the tent as all turned toward him. "Brothers and Sisters, we have a new friend in our midst today. Won't you please make him welcome." Then he looked to me and said, "Brother, won't you please rise and introduce yourself to your new friends?"

All attention turned back to me. The heat of their anticipation made me cower in my seat.

Time stopped. Then, with a will of their own, my legs raised my reluctant body from the bench. I stood there, motionless, uneasy, unable to move, wilting under their stares. I had no words.

Again, Brother Joseph's voice coaxed, "Brother, please, won't you tell us your name?"

I turned toward his voice. My eyes lifted toward the stage.

Seated beside him on the stage was a beautiful young woman. She wore a white dress with small red flowers. She had the prettiest, curliest yellow hair I'd ever seen.

A worn mandolin lay on her lap.

She raised her head.

Our eyes met.

She lifted the mandolin and held it to her chest.

Tears began to burn my cheeks.

I could see tears on her cheeks too.

Then I heard a voice.

It was my voice.

"My name is Russell Jordan; folks call me Rusty!"

Chapter 24

*M*ary sat in the back seat with me. Brother Joseph drove the car to-ward West Plains, followed by a truck that carried the tent and all their materials. Brother Joseph, the boy I knew as Joey, was now an associate pastor in a church there. He shared a preaching ministry that stretched across Southern Missouri and Northern Arkansas.

Mary still held her mandolin and began asking a million questions–questions I could not yet answer out loud. I soon realized that I had never told them about Janie, or the farm in Iowa or running away, or anything. And in light of what had just happened in Hidden Spring, I needed to think, to sort it all. I had my own questions–fundamental questions like–Why has this all happened to me? Is there a greater meaning to all this? Has my life been directed by fate, or something larger? I had no answers for myself or Mary.

They put my stuff in the spare bedroom of the parsonage. "Stay with us," Mary pleaded. "Joey and I are so happy to have you back. We prayed every day for your return. Please tell me you are here to stay. You poor thing. Tomorrow we will get you all cleaned up and get you some nicer clothes."

I woke to the smell of hot coffee and freshly baked rolls. Bleary-eyed, I entered the bright, cozy kitchen where Mary was happily working at her oven and preparing the table, all while humming aloud. Joey sat with his back to me, reading his Bible. "Good morning Rusty. Did you have a restful night?"

Before I could speak, Mary turned, slid to my side, and hugged me. "It is so wonderful to have you here. It's been so long, but I never gave up hope. Sit here and tell us everything," she said, setting a cup of coffee in front of me.

It was easier for me to talk today. I started at the beginning. I told about the farm, Mama, Janie, and Mr. Webster. I told them about the day the man and woman had stolen Janie, about how I went to Fairfield, searching. I told them about leaving the farm and how I ended up at the General Store door, begging. I didn't tell them about the man in the truck. I had never told anyone about that day and never would.

I told them about being overwhelmed by Miriam's illness, then about Ray giving me the store. I told them about leaving in the middle of the night because I couldn't stay and didn't have the courage to face them.

"Why didn't you tell us?" Mary begged.

"I was too young to understand. I didn't know what was driving me away, and I couldn't explain it, even to myself. I knew I would cry and I didn't want to see either of you suffer," I said.

We sat silently for several minutes, lost in our thoughts. Joey finally spoke, "The past is the past, nothing can be done to change it. It is only alive in our thoughts. I believe the Lord has brought you back to us for a reason. Now we can only rejoice and look to the future."

Chapter 25

$\mathcal{J}$oey helped me find a job with a local carpentry shop, West Plains Carpentry. It had a small apartment attached, so the owner, Robert Crandall, let me live there as part of my wages. He extended his hand, smiled broadly, and said, "Please call me Bob."

His business was remodeling homes, building small buildings like garages and storage sheds, and building furniture and small specialty items like picture frames. I didn't know much about remodeling and shed building, but it was nice to be around the sweet smell of wood again. In just weeks, Bob and I developed a friendship. He was glad to have someone eager to help and I felt at ease, working with someone who required nothing more from me than a willingness to work.

It wasn't long before word began to spread about the new guy at the carpentry shop, and Bob's specialty business began to grow. This meant I spent less time at worksites and more in the shop. Bob was happy about the new business and I was willing to work on-site whenever I was needed. I began to settle in. In my slow times, I built lawn furniture like gliders, porch swings, and benches which we displayed around the building. Mary and I soon began to spend evenings on a glider that she picked as her favorite. "Please don't sell this one," she said. "We should keep it as 'our place.' You can tell customers that it is for display only."

I had a stove and refrigerator in the apartment but only fixed breakfast myself. Mary was there every evening, either bringing me dinner or fixing it while I drank tea at the table and watched.

One evening, Joey came with Mary and we had dinner together at the table. Joey said, "I've been thinking about your sister, Janie. Brother David, Brother William and I alternate our preaching mission every month. One of us is on the road tent-preaching the gospel, while the other two stay here to shepherd our flock. We travel over southern Missouri and Northern Arkansas. Sometimes we are called as far as parts of Kansas,

Oklahoma, Kentucky, and Mississippi. We preach to thousands of people every year.

"Brother William mentioned we could look for Janie by making and distributing posters. We would put them at the tent entrances and mention her after our sermons. We could also post the signs, with permission, in store windows. Police stations might be willing to paste them on their walls. I talked to The Quill–our newspaper–and they said they would be glad to print them for us."

"I could help," Mary said. "I go with Joey almost every time. I would be glad to talk to people, pass out the posters to stores, police stations, courthouses and anyplace else we could think of. Jenny, Brother David's wife, will help too, I know she will."

"We just need to design a poster, Rusty. What do you think?" Joey asked.

"I wish I had thought of this before. I think of all the places where I could have left posters," I answered.

The next Tuesday, Brother David and his wife left on their month-long mission to preach in places they were called west of West Plains. They pulled a trailer loaded with the tent and on the seat between them lay a package of posters.

I watched until they disappeared over the top of the hill on the east edge of town. At least maybe this time there is a chance.

PLEASE HELP US FIND
A MISSING GIRL
JANIE JORDAN

BLOND HAIR
BLUE EYES
APPROXIMATELY
22 YEARS OF AGE
LAST SEEN IN
SOUTHEAST IOWA OVER
15 YEARS AGO
PLEASE CONTACT

THE WEST PLAINS QUILL

WEST PLAINS, MO
NO QUESTIONS ASKED

Every Saturday morning I walked downtown to The Quill's office to ask Cleo, the editor if there was any news. At first, she was happy to see me. But as the weeks wore on and she never received any word, she began to dread my arrival. Her discomfort soon made it harder for me to ask. I knew if she received any word, a rumor even, she would hurry to bring me the message. I began to skip my Saturday walks, knowing there would be no news. I didn't like seeing the uncomfortable expression on Cleo's face.

One evening, sitting on the bench in front of the carpenter shop, I broke the silence, "Mary, when I came back to Hidden Spring, I stopped at the General Store before walking into town. I saw my Rusty's Repair sign leaning against the front wall and it looked like it had been cleaned recently. Then, when I walked out to the garden, I was stunned to someone had beenb tending to the flowers and cleaning Miriam's bench. There was even one of her tablecloths folded and laying over the end."

Mary blushed, "I told you I never gave up hope. Every time Joey and I go preaching for a month, we always go west. Then, either going out or coming back or both, we stop in Hidden Spring at the General Store. I tend to the flowers while Joey sits on the bench. Each time, before we leave, I hang a fresh tablecloth over the end of the bench, just like Miriam did. Then Joey sits in Ray's chair and I clean your sign. Before we leave we pray for your safety, wherever you may be," she said.

"But that is just every third month, does it always look like that?" I asked.

"I know, I haven't had a chance to tell you. Mom takes care of it too. She has finally gotten over Daddy dying. She doesn't drink anymore and has a boyfriend, Jim. Jim works for Mr. McDowell at his new hardware store and runs Mr. Hickenbottom's sawmill. He has fixed up Mom's place and they go to church together. Every Sunday afternoon they walk up the hill and he helps her tend Miriam's flowers. If there are any to pick, she brings one bloom home and keeps it in a vase on her table. She is so thankful that you helped Joey and me when she couldn't." Her eyes filled with tears as she said, "I told you we never gave up."

On one of their first missions to the west, Joey and Mary had brought back the Rusty's Repair sign and asked Bob if he would hang it on the front of the shop under his sign. They said, "Rusty would like that." He readily agreed. That cheered me up a little, but it had been over a year since they had begun distributing posters, yet we had not received any response about Janie. I avoided The Quill now. Whenever I met her on the street or in a store, she would ask if I had received any news, but it was just a courtesy; we both knew she would be the first to hear if there ever was any. The three pastors kept telling me not to give up, that someday we would learn something. But even Mary mentioned Janie's name less frequently.

I quietly began to build an inventory of extra swings, gliders, and lawn chairs. I finished all the complicated repair jobs in the shop. I quit shaving and getting haircuts. I told Bob that I would be leaving soon and asked him not to tell anyone. I wrote thank-you notes to Cleo, Brother William, and Brother David.

After dinner, Mary and I were sitting on the porch, swinging as usual. Joey was sitting in the rocker. I was watching huge cumulus clouds pass through the sky, occasionally blocking the sun. I was quiet, thinking, wondering, can Janie see the same clouds I see?

"Rusty," Mary said.

I didn't respond, my mind was still wandering.

"Rusty, you haven't shaved for a while," she said.

I rubbed the stubble on my chin.

"Rusty, we know you are leaving. Will you please say goodbye this time before you go?"

Mary squeezed my hand as she rose. I watched as she walked away. She didn't look back.

I went back to my room and sat on the bed. I was quietly trying to make sense of it all when I heard a knock on the door. "Rusty, it's Bob. Brother Joseph told me you are leaving tonight. I wish you wouldn't, but I understand why you think you must. I will miss you. You are the best helper I have ever had. But more than a helper—you have become a great friend. I want you to know that if you ever come back, I will have a place for you. Good-bye and good luck, my friend."

Later that evening, I took my suitcase from the closet and walked to the bus depot, and boarded with a tickct taking me west.

Chapter 26

*S*everal days later, a young lady knocked on the West Plains Carpentry door. Mary, who had spent most of her time there lately, answered. "Yes?" she said as she opened the door.

"Hello, my name is Eve Miller. Is there a Rusty here?" she asked.

"No, I am sorry, Rusty isn't here," Mary answered.

"Do you know when he will be back?" Eve asked.

"No, I don't. He has left. He didn't leave any forwarding information. We don't know when he will be back," Mary said. "Is there something I can help you with?"

"I live in Springfield. A girlfriend of mine grew up here in West Plains. She was back visiting family a week ago and when she got back, she told me she had seen the Rusty's Repair sign on your building."

"Won't you please come in?" Mary asked. "Can I offer you something to drink, sweet tea, water, a soda?"

They sat at the table with their drinks.

Mary began, "Why are you interested in Rusty and the sign?"

"I lived in an orphanage in Springfield when I was a small child. They told me my name is Eve Miller, but I don't think that is my real name. When I was little, I lived on a small farm somewhere, with who I think was my mother and brother. I don't know what my mother's name was, but I remember my brother's name was Rusty. I think they called me Jane."

Mary began to weep uncontrollably.

"Did I say something wrong?" Eve begged.

"No. The Rusty you are looking for was here. He lived here for over a year but left only two days ago. Your real name is Janie Jordan." Mary cried.

"We don't know where he went or when he will come back. We don't know if he will ever come back. He was gone for almost ten years before he came here. Before that, he lived in Hidden Spring for several years. That is where I met him. He has spent his whole life looking for you. If only this were a week ago!" Mary said.

They sat, sobbed, and held each other.

"Are you my sister?" Janie asked.

"No, but we look alike, don't we?" Mary smiled, forcing a laugh.

"I have hoped for so long that Rusty and I could someday find each other, and now, to come this close. I don't know what to do," Janie cried.

"Let me call my brother. He is a minister. He can help and he will want to meet you. He will know what to do," Mary said.

She took her arms from around Janie and hurried to the phone. "Gertie," she told the operator, "this is Mary. Would you please connect me with the church? I need to speak to Brother Joseph."

"Joey, please come to the carpenter shop. I need you here right now," she pleaded the instant he answered.

"Are you hurt?" Joey asked.

"No, I'm not hurt," she said.

"Brother David and I are in a meeting with the church board. I'll be there in about forty-five minutes."

"You need to come here now. Right now!" Mary shouted.

The instant Joey arrived, Mary jumped and ran to him. "Joey, this is Janie!" she cried.

After the hugs and tears subsided, they sat at the kitchen table where Janie began a long story that Mary and Joey didn't dare interrupt...

"I remember leaving in a car with a man and a woman. I didn't understand why Rusty wasn't going with me. They took me to a big house in a big town where there were a lot of other kids, mostly around my age. The girls there all stayed together in a couple of big rooms. The boys all stayed in the basement."

"Some of the ladies that took care of us were nice, but the woman who was in charge and her helper were mean. Her name was Miss Raschid.

"We got punished all the time, mostly for little things like leaving a drawer open or not cleaning the tables good enough. I soon realized we were in an adoption home and everyone in there except some of the bigger kids would be sent to homes somewhere. Usually, the mean kids, the dumber ones or the ones who were brought back, worked there because they either were too old, or no one wanted them.

"All we had were ragged old clothes that didn't fit. I never did have any shoes. We slept on cots that were in rows around the walls of the big rooms. There were times when there were more kids than cots, so the new kids had to sleep on the floor. They taught us all to read and write and speak correctly. The girls helped in the kitchen, learned how to cook. The boys all worked outside. They tried to teach us all good manners.

"When people came to look at us, the helpers made us bathe and gave us nice clothes to wear. That was the only time I wore shoes.

"I guess the people that came were looking for some specific child like a boy a particular age with freckles, or a girl with blond hair; something like that. The younger kids always seemed to get picked first. I guess I was lucky because I only went on parade three or four times. That is what they called it when we walked in front of the people who came there wanting to adopt.

"A couple named Sheila and Harry took me. She was nice, but I didn't like him. He would touch me when Sheila wasn't around. I lived with them in a big house in a huge city. I later learned I was in Dallas, Texas.

"It was a nice house and I had nice clothes, but I hated being there. I was the only child in the house. I guess I cried a lot at first. Harry didn't like that and was constantly yelling at Sheila about what a mistake I was. As I got older, Harry got meaner, and he was touching me more. Eventually, Sheila got frustrated with me and gave in to Harry's demands to get rid of me. Then they brought me back to the orphanage.

"Then I was too big to be wanted by anyone else so I became one of the helpers. The female helpers had a room on the top floor. We couldn't leave without permission and they hardly ever gave anyone permission. There was a big fence around the yard so no one could sneak out.

"Every day I thought about Rusty and Mama and the farm, but I didn't know how to get out, or how to find him. I didn't even know where the farm was.

"One day I was standing in my upstairs window looking out and saw a red-headed boy standing between two older ladies. They were at the fence looking at the kids in the playground. I got a strange feeling inside like I was going to get sick, only it was a good sick. My heart started pounding, 'could it be?' I thought. I ran down the steps past Mrs. Raschid, who tried to stop me, and out into the playground. By the time I got there, the boy and the two ladies were gone.

"I stood in that window every day after, every chance I got, but they never came back.

"I became good friends with one of the other helpers, a girl named Mary who was about my age. She had never been an orphan, so Mrs. Raschid treated her better than the rest of us. Several weeks ago she got permission to visit her family. Her mom and dad live here in West Plains. I had told her everything I knew about me, so when she saw the Rusty's Repair sign above the door here, she told me about it when she got back. I watched the front door of the orphanage until two days ago when the headmistress left her desk to go to the restroom, then I fled through the front door." Janie finished, as she wiped away another tear.

"Joey, what are we going to do?" asked Mary.

"Pray for guidance," he answered.

"Janie, you can stay in our spare bedroom as long as you like. We will find Rusty; it surely must be the Lord's will," he told her.

He turned to Mary, "Let's get all the posters we have printed, get red crayons from the Sunday school supplies and write something like, 'JANIE HAS BEEN FOUND' across them. We will send some to each police station or church we can think of. You call the newspaper and ask if they can print more posters with those words in color for us. I'll get the ladies' Queen Esther group to write on all the posters we have and do the ones the paper prints for us if they can't print in color. Brother William is in the field; we can find his location and mail him new posters. I will ask the congregation for a special offering to pay for the printing and shipping," Joey finally took a breath and then continued with determination.

"Then I will talk to Brother David. He can stay here, minister the church and offer guidance in our search. I'll take posters and travel to every location west of here, put them in all the police stations along the way and ask each church for their help. Every poster we find, we will write that Janie has been found. We will need all the brightly colored crayons we can find.

Turning to Mary, Joey concluded, "You can stay here and care for Janie; help her in any way. There are probably many things that will need to be done from here that I can't think of now. And most of all, pray," he said.

Chapter 27

I got off the bus at Eureka Springs. I had a ticket to ride farther but the bus would stop in Springfield and I didn't want to go there. Once again I was going but didn't know where. I had spent a year in West Plains. I liked it there. I could spend the rest of my life there, but we had found no trace of Janie despite all that Joey and Mary had done. I couldn't stay. I realized that if I continued in this direction, I would go through Springfield or maybe on into the desolate west. I didn't want either; I decided to turn north. As much as I didn't like big cities, I thought maybe Des Moines or Omaha might be places to look.

I hitched a ride with a couple of boys–Doug and Tommy–who had been working for the CCC in the Ozark mountains. They were going home to Cassville, Missouri for the weekend. When we got there, they let me out downtown and drove away to their homes. I found a café, ate lunch, and spent the rest of the day sitting on a park bench, thinking and wondering. It was too late in the day to travel any further. I would have to stay here. Cassville didn't have a hotel or motor park, so I found a tree in the park and spread my sleeping bag.

A bright light shining in my eyes woke me. "Whatcha doin' here, boy?" he growled.

"I'm just passing through, officer. I just stopped for the night," I told him.

"Where ya from? Ya got someplace yer goin'?" he asked.

"No, sir. I'm just traveling," I said.

"Got a home or a destination?"

"No, sir."

"Well, here in Cassville, we call guys like you vagrants. We kinda think of vagrants as bums. We don't like no bums hangin' round here. Git in my squad car, boy. I'm gonna let you spend the rest a yer night in one of our city's finest cells. Tomorrow, ya git to talk to the judge, before I ride you to the edge of town and dump you out," he snapped.

I had never been in jail before and didn't like it. They put me in a cell next to a drunk who moaned all night about how mean his wife was to him. At least he had a wife and home.

The next morning, standing in front of the judge wasn't any better.

"We don't like vagrants here, son. I'm going to sentence you to one more day in jail; then we will give you your stuff and we are going to have you leave Cassville. If I ever have you standing before me again, your sentence will be a month cutting weeds for the county and sleeping in a cell," he said.

The following morning, I begged a different officer to take me to the bus depot. There I bought a ticket to Joplin.

"I called the bus station, Joey," Mary said. "The man told me Rusty bought a ticket to Springfield. I called the bus station in Springfield and they said he wasn't on the bus when it arrived," Mary said. "They are trying to find the bus driver, but Springfield was his last stop. He didn't stay overnight at the hotel. They are trying to find out if he has relatives there or whether he may have piggybacked on another bus. I explained why we wanted to know. They said they would do all they could."

Joplin was a bigger town than I thought it would be. I found a phone booth in the lobby of a hotel. Joplin had several orphanages and children's homes. I rented a room for the week. Early the next morning, I sat with the phone book and made a list of places to visit. I wished we had thought of Joplin that first time I came to Springfield with Ray and Miriam.

The first place, a Baptist mission and children's home on the west side of town, didn't seem promising but they were friendly and sympathetic. They were willing to share their records once I explained. The lady asked me when my sister was stolen. I told her it was about fifteen years ago. She said, "Oh, we are looking for a young lady then." Again it dawned on me that Janie would be all grown up by now. I'm not looking for a little girl anymore; I'm looking for a young woman. Maybe this is why she is so cooperative.

From now on, I'll make sure whoever I talk to understands that this happened a long time ago.

Unfortunately, their records only went back for ten years.

"We had a lady, Mrs. Magruder, that was in charge here for years. She may recall something. I could visit with her next time she comes to Joplin. She has a son here. Where can I reach you if I find something about your sister?" she asked.

"I don't have a home. I will check with you in a few weeks."

She lowered her head in understanding. "Good luck to you, sir," she said as I left.

The next morning, I went to the Presbyterian Home for Children. They explained they only process children for the church diocese, so they don't keep records. I would have to contact each church individually. The minister gave me a list of all the churches in their network. There were more than thirty.

My last hope here was the Apostolic Home for Orphans. Mr. Hickenbottom was the manager of their orphanage. He gave me a record book that went back almost thirty years. "Take as long as you like, Rusty. Our quilting ladies will be here today. They always have a small potluck at noon; you are welcome to join them. I am sure they would love to hear your story; they know more about the goings-on in Joplin than anyone. They might be able to help," he said.

I was uncomfortable sharing my story with strangers, but they weren't strangers long. Once I finished, I was engulfed in sympathy and hugs. There were offers of places to stay, food and clothes for my search, leads for me to follow, and money. They took a collection right then and insisted I take it. It was embarrassing, but it came from good souls. I reluctantly accepted.

I returned to the hotel with a list of names and phone numbers and a wad of money. Only three calls seemed promising. I planned to meet with them the next day.

Two families were in Springfield; both had pictures. None were of Janie.

The third lead was in Sarcoxie. I bought a round-trip bus ticket the next morning.

"Hello, can I help you?" a gray-haired little man said through his screen door.

I explained, "I am looking for my sister who may have passed through the Springfield Apostolic Orphanage about fifteen years ago. I met with the quilting club ladies a couple of days ago. They gave me your name as someone who may have some knowledge about her."

He led me through a living room cluttered with stacks of newspapers and books. The tables were covered with candles, clocks, and old pictures. There was a pipe stand or ashtray at every chair and couch. "Haven't had a chance to straighten up for a while," he apologized.

I followed him into a dimly lit study with walls lined with shelves. I had never seen such disarray–so many stacks of stuff. He removed some of the clutter and tunneled to a broken wooden box with its lid missing. He turned to me, cradling the treasure. "If I got anything, it's in here," he said, as he handed it to me. "If you got any questions just ask."

The box was stuffed with old photographs. Most were torn, had been folded, or were wrinkled. None had anything written on the back. I sat at his desk and began. Most I set aside at first glance– pictures of men and women, older folks, houses, farms, ships, and mountains–all without a note. When I did find a picture of a girl, no matter the age, he would look over my shoulder and say, "Yeah, that's so and so." He'd give a name, where she once lived, who her parents were. It struck me that these photos held meaning only to him and the people in them. When he took that knowledge with him to his grave, it would be gone forever. Twice I found blond girls that he couldn't identify. "Don't know how they got in there; you can take them with if you like?" he said.

I put each in my pocket.

After almost three hours, I rose from the box. "Thank you very much for your time," I said. "You have been most considerate."

"Enjoyed it myself," he smiled. "I don't get to talk to young'uns much. Sorry I couldn't be more help. I wish you luck in your search. What'd you say your name was again?"

"Folks call me Rusty, sir," I answered. "It was a pleasure to meet you."

"No need to call me sir, Rusty. Folks round these parts call me Smiley. Never did know why; making fun of me, I guess. I don't mind, they can call me anything they want, long's they call me for supper," he laughed.

It was only two o'clock, almost four hours until the bus back to Joplin. With nothing more to do, I bought a soda and began to explore. I walked to the west edge of town, discovered the cemetery, and mindlessly walked among the stones. In a few hours, I would catch the bus back to Joplin. Tonight, my last night in my room, I would lay in bed, wondering. Tomorrow, I would rise, pack my stuff, and travel on. But where would I go? Where next? And why? For over fifteen years I had been moving, searching, hiding, denying. And for what? For this? I am standing in the middle of a cemetery in Sarcoxie, Missouri with no hope and nowhere to go.

I trudged back through town toward the bus depot. My mind was spinning–not spinning–then spinningagain. I didn't know what to do now. I was just lost and confused. All my hope was gone.

As I walked toward the depot I passed the police station. A ray of sunshine broke through the overcast sky. The reflection from it caused the station window to light up. Something caused me to look toward the window. Inside I saw posters cluttering a bulletin board. One of the posters caught my eye. It looked like one that Joey, Mary, and the Brothers had distributed, but it wasn't quite the same. It had red markings on it. I stepped over, cupped my hands to the glass, and looked in.

Written over the front of the poster in red crayon were the words:

RUSTY COME BACK! WE FOUND JANIE!

**PLEASE HELP US FIND
A MISSING GIRL
JANIE JORDAN**

**BLOND HAIR
BLUE EYES
APPROXIMATELY
22 YEARS OF AGE
LAST SEEN IN
SOUTHEAST IOWA OVER
15 YEARS AGO
PLEASE CONTACT**

**THE WEST PLAINS QUILL
WEST PLAINS, MO
NO QUESTIONS ASKED**

RUSTY COME BACK

WE FOUND

JANIE!

EPILOGUE

*I*n West Plains, Missouri, out past the Country Club on old 160 Highway, and nestled in a grove of white oak trees, sits a log cabin home with a red tin roof. A new barn with a matching roof sits just to the side and a little behind. A young couple with curly red-headed twin boys lives there.

A sign stands next to the street. It reads:

RUSTY'S WOODSHOP

CUSTOM FURNITURE MADE AND REPAIRED

There is always a display of homemade furniture on the cabin's porch. Usually, a dining suite, consisting of a table and chairs and a matching hutch or buffet, made from either red oak or maple, sitting on one side. An ever-changing row of chairs and gliders sit on the other. Mostly they are rocking chairs made from red oak, white oak, sycamore, poplar, walnut, or elm. An older worn chair sits between the two displays, next to the front door. A sign on the wall above it simply says, NOT FOR SALE. A glider sits next to it with the words, FOR DISPLAY ONLY.

Strangely, only children are drawn to them.

Two freshly restored antique Standard Oil gas pumps, Red Crown, and Gold Crown sit under a canopy out front. A small, immaculately kept flower garden sits just off the far corner of the porch. A large homemade bench occupies a spot amid the roses, irises, and daylilies. Most days, if you pass about two p. m., you will see a woman sitting in the glider, swinging back and forth as she plays her mandolin. She sits, singing and watching her boys racing their rocking horses in the yard. Sometimes a second young woman will be there, swinging in the glider, singing in harmony. Passersby often stop to watch and listen.

Every Saturday at precisely 4:00 p. m., the owner of the shop turns off the lights and locks the front door. He walks a few steps, then turns and gazes at his shop. He smiles, removes his hat, and bows his head for an instant, seemingly in reverence to a worn Rusty's Repair sign that hangs above the door, and what it must mean to him.

Also, precisely at 4:00 p.m., his wife spreads a freshly-pressed but faded yellow tablecloth–with red, pink, and orange flowers around the edges– over a bench in the flower garden. A few minutes later her brother, a local minister, and his wife arrive with their curly, blonde-headed twin daughters. The two women spread a blanket on the ground next to the garden for the children. The two sets of twins enjoy a tray of steaming, freshly baked cookies and glasses of cold milk.

The four adults–Joey and Janie, Rusty and Mary–sit quietly on the bench watch their children and savor their fresh muffins and glasses of iced tea.

About the Author

Roger K. Droz was born and raised in Fairfield, Iowa. He graduated from Parsons College with a BA in History and Political Science.

He had a short story, "Bikes and Basketball," published in *Our Iowa Magazine* and another short story, "First Beer," was the winner of the Creative Nonfiction category of the 2016 Kansas Voices contest.

Roger currently resides in Topeka, Kansas with his wife, Margo. *Rusty's Repair* is his debut novel.